AF662947

The Girl From The WOODS

notionpress
.com

The Girl From The WOODS

AMAR SHEKHAR

notionpress.com

Notion Press

5 Muthu Kalathy Street, Triplicane,

Chennai - 600 005

First Published by Notion Press 2015

Copyright © Amar Shekhar 2015

All Rights Reserved.

ISBN: 978-93-52060-65-8

This book has been published in good faith that the work of the author is original. All efforts have been taken to make the material error-free. However, the author and the publisher disclaim the responsibility.

No part of this book may be used, reproduced in any manner whatsoever without written permission from the author, except in the case of brief quotations embodied in critical articles and reviews.

To my mother and family
To all the adventurers

Thanks to:

Sushmita Jain, for being the first reader and editor of my manuscript at all the stages in writing of this book. She was always there to guide me on days, nights, weekends, and holidays.

HardyHawks team: Vaibhav singh Rajput, Anand Verma and Neeldhwaj Pathak, for sharing my dreams and motivating me to follow my passion.

Anand Shekhar, my brother, whose poems have always been a motivation to me.

My mother, sister and family, for their love, kindness and care.

Alexander Rau, for providing me a space to turn my dream into reality and making sure that I always had a comfortable stay in Berlin while writing this book.

Abhinav Pundir, for being my elder brother.

Amrita Pal, for her great comments in the final stage of the manuscript.

Tobias, Nadine, Christian, Sophie, Mo and Shayan for spending great times with me.

My friends, for your love.

My amazing trek mates, for being a part of my adventure journey.

My extended family on my blog and social media.

Notion Press, for publishing me.

And, dear readers for putting trust in me.

Contents

SHIMLA

"See, golden apples!" she clutched my right arm as she pointed to a bunch of golden apples displayed at the front of a shop.

"I thought you wanted to shoot them. So...," she stopped.

I looked at her and smiled. She looked a little shy and childish at the satme time. She looked at me like an innocent child, as though she had tried to express an innocent message with her compelling eyes. She also smiled at me in return. Whenever she smiled, her cheeks bloomed red and its radiance lit up every corner of her face as if the sun had descended down from the sky and made her face its home. It fit perfectly in line with the bang which peeked out from under the round white fur cap she wore.

Well, now it is time to tell you something about myself. I admire nature and find solace in lonely places. I want to turn to nature because humanity does not interest me anymore. I have had some painful experiences with the people around me. I stopped seeking humanity in the beings that are left on this mundane earth. Well, maybe I sound like a sadist and I suppose I do have my own faults too. I agree. But, I would say that I always have had a tendency to renounce what most would consider the norm. I have been trying hard to indulge in self-actualization. By taking cues from the past and in evaluating my habits, I found out that my soul belonged to nature more than to anything else. Nature, anyway, is eventually where everything else belongs!

I can sit for hours waiting to capture a perfect shot of the sunset. Yeah, it should tell you a lot about me. I am headstrong, but I am more passionate than being a headstrong. I am a survivor, and have been this way since childhood. I believe very strongly that I can persevere through any situation. The more challenging the situation is; the more fun it seems to me.

Eventually, I found something that suited my interests. I found a job that was best-suited for me. Everyone else would agree too. My passion for the wild and writing pages and pages about the beauty of nature landed me a job of my liking. I am a wildlife enthusiast, an amateur photographer and a free soul writer, who earns his bread and butter from nature. People like to read my stories and enjoy seeing my photographs from every tour I undertake. I go to offbeat locations, to seasonal places and to wild locations. I photograph the scenery, the raw beauty of nature and the wilderness. I meet new people; I write stories and courier them to big offices made of concrete, glass and bricks in the city. My way of life has earned me a few admirers, a few followers and many friends across the country. One thing I have always been afraid of, though, is love. I did have a healthy love life, but none of my affairs have worked and remained steadfast in the past.

This is how my story begins – with a trip to Shimla, which left a major footprint in my memory, a footprint that would last forever.

I got down at Kalka and took a look around. There were long shadows that fell over the brown sloppy grass. Narrow rail-gauges merged. The lone toy train plying in the region had left a while ago. I admired the picturesque setting, wondering if I had entered another world without realizing that. I smiled and began to walk slowly, thinking and marveling at how I was on a journey of drifting away and getting lost in the vast portals of beauty. I was forsaking my existence. I was abandoning my corrupted memories accumulated over past few months. And I was working to rejuvenate my withered self with the boundless happiness that was hanging onto every tree. Every dusty step I was going to take was taking me towards shedding my old self. I had just come out of the pits. I was going to Shimla, where I would shoot scenes set in the cold wilderness for a month – right in the middle of a harsh winter and I would try to restart my life.

I put my luggage into a taxi and set off. There were two ways to reach Shimla: the conventional and the unconventional way. I chose the latter. I was least interested in a crowded street or in shopping on the streets. I wanted to explore the wild in its natural setting, while carrying my personal peace along. I was ahead of schedule. I had reached Kalka a day before and decided to stay at Dharampur before leaving for Shimla the next morning. Visiting Dharampur gave me a chance to explore, and look for a place for my mind to rest. The little town was reminiscent of British-India. Wooden houses with sloping roofs, narrow streets, and old fashioned buildings created an old-worldly charm. The hotel rooms were old-fashioned, too. I looked around in search of a quiet place – and I was sure I wouldn't have found it in a market. I was directed to a Gurudwara, but it turned out to be a private space that I could not use. I checked in at a shelter situated just off the highway. It was an old wooden cottage that was renovated to suit modern needs. A maroon carpet was laid out from the entrance, leading into the rooms. My heavy boots thumped the wooden steps loudly. The room I was allotted was big enough for one person to sleep in – but that too, only if he curled up in bed. I set my things down in the room and opened the window. I heard a familiar sound from outside – the toy train chugged and puffed in the distance. I rushed to my bag and took out my camera. I love my relationship with my camera – it shoots exactly what I envision. I followed the toy train through the lens, as it crawled through the pine trees and gleamed in the afternoon sun. It turned at the edge of the valley. It had big wooden windows. I saw a few people looking outside their windows. The toy train gradually crawled behind the hill and went out of sight. I set my camera aside, took off my shoes and jumped onto the bed. After a few rounds of visuals, I decided to go for a walk. As I stepped outside, the cold wind blew across, whispering in my ears. I strolled along the portico of the cottage. I took in the sights and sounds of Dharampur, and the small chain of hills beyond. The hills looked dark, in shades of brown with a few green patches in places. In the evenings, as I would later see for myself, the hills wore a coat of a thousand colors, glinting and shining in the radiance of the setting sun. At around seven, I drew back the curtains and peeped out. The small town looked sleepy glowing silently under the gleam of the yellow street lights. A few lights were scattered across the hills, but the highway to Shimla was still alive. I filled a bucket full of hot water and sat down with my legs soaking in it, while reading a novel. After every few pages that I read, I would stare into the darkness outside or fasten my gaze on the wall for some time lost pondering in the thoughts. As time passed and darkness engulfed all around, I felt closer to the lost part of the wanderlust that thrived within me. It was a vacuum and soundlessness all around. It was an adrift life that carried me away to another tranquil dreamland.

I got up the next day and took another taxi to Shimla, following the path that was flanked by the wilderness. I took the seventy kilometers road that was long and circuitous. It had three wildlife sanctuaries on the way. I went past two of the most famous hill stations of Lower Himachal and enjoyed the view of an open river restaurant and the world's highest cricket ground on the way.

As one leaves the Kalka-Shimla highway behind at Kandaghat and takes a right turn towards Chail, there is another world awaiting the visitor. You are no longer driving along a broad highway. This road is narrow and allows only one vehicle to pass through at a time, in some places. There are sharp twists and turns along the serpentine Himalayan road. One must go slow while on the curves, blow a horn and use a dipper at night. Sometimes, the road gets so narrow that one might have to follow a slow moving lorry for a stretch of a kilometer or two, but these annoyances are paid for with interest. The returns come in the form of tranquility and the beauty of nature. As one enters the route, they are welcomed by the slopes that are beset with Deodar trees, pine trees, oak trees and the like. These dense trees covered the slopes to the left of the road to Chail and on the right, there flowed a river. At some places, trees were so dense that the road appeared to meeting an end. Along the river there were small huts and cottages. The huts housed farm owners. They were mostly terrace-farmers and step-farmers, working along the slopes of the hills. As we sped along the roads, we slowly lost sight of the river as the forest began to get denser. As we inched towards Chail, the forests got denser and the number of people on the roads grew fewer. Thanks to the thick and dense foliage, it got darker and the road ahead seemed obscure. It got scarier when the sun set and an avalanche of fog hovered over the clouds, making the roads more slippery and wetter. It felt one would feel like he was driving through a deserted village that had overgrown shrubbery everywhere. I heard that it got darker at night. Towards Kufri, luckier ones might encounter Himalayan panthers, Himalayan black bears, wild cats, jackals, barking deer and sometimes, even the Himachali Ghoral, on the way through the Chail wildlife sanctuary.

Sometimes, it gets darker and foggier even during the day that one has to turn on the vehicle's fog lights and wipers on. As one heads to Kufri, the Chail wildlife sanctuary awaits. On a sunny day, it is possible to see the length and breadth of the Himalayan ranges at the horizon, driving along the high roads. The road from Kufri to Shimla joins the Ambala-Shimla highway after passing Kufri, and then passes through the Shimla Reserve Forest Sanctuary.

Finally, I reached Shimla at a time when it was in the throes of a very harsh winter. It snowed relentlessly, and for weeks on end, the sun remained unseen. Traffic hit stops on occasion, and tourists found themselves stranded. Thanks to the demands of my assignment, I was booked free accommodation from my club. Soon, I would be given my work-lot, which would comprise a four by four vehicle, a map of the areas I needed to cover, camping gears, a list of people I could contact in the areas around where I was going to work, and my photography kit.

Thanks to heavy snowfall, it took long for the lot to arrive. Without anything else to do, I wandered aimlessly on the streets, and explored the markets. I spent time with the locals and listened to the stories about themselves and the places around. I lazed around and lost track of time. The weather forecast predicted that Shimla was in line for heavy snowfall. It reminded me of the Berlin's snowfall. Snowflakes fell gently all day long from the dark-grey clouds. They then aggressively took over the streets, valleys, hills, woods and everything that got in line. The snowflakes looked like little crystalline balls of sugar mixed with white cotton – looking incredibly beautiful, like a transparent water crystal hanging precariously off the fur of a cap. Walking against the cold wind tempted me often to open my mouth and eat some of the snowflakes. The flakes invariably settled down on the ground, like nomads in early France. Sometimes, vehicles sped over the roads, leaving dirt tracks in the snow. Watching the city turn into a white world was like a dream.

The window in my room gave me my best solo and abstract prints: lonely streets, big yellow lights burning in the dark, gloomy sunsets and dark cold nights. Before opening the window, I would guess about the weather outside, based on the hazy images of the outside world through the one-inch thick translucent glass. With time, I developed a strong fondness for the window, so much so that the first thing I did when I entered my room was to stand by it and gaze outside, accounting for the changes in the world beyond the glass. But, little did I know that the same glass would open up a world of sweet troubles for me. A series of unseen events were already waiting for me, events which would bend the flow of my life; events that would annul the beliefs that I held sacredly in my mind; events that would force me to rethink every upshot and events that would want me to reconfigure my whole life.

She

I saw her first in the woods across the hotel window. She was taller than usual girls. Though I was not a face-reader or some sort of face-connoisseur but I could guess that her face was a heart-shaped in golden ratio. I loved looking at her face especially when she peered innocently out of aligned bangs lying carelessly on her forehead. She just looked like a child who was lately woken up from her sleep. Her innocent eyes were always enigmatic to me. Though they always looked overt but they also concealed some abstruse quandaries behind them. Sometimes her eyes presented me my pseudo-shadow where I saw myself without any veil of worldly attributes. That shadow was a doppelgänger who was an immaculate version of my existence. Most of the times, she was outspoken. She loved to talk like a child and ask as many questions as she could. Often she came so much closer tattling to my ears that it made me laugh.

The deserted forests looked black in the harsh winter, but it still had some contrasts. Though they lacked beauty, they seemed to symbolize hope. Soon, it would be spring, and the snow-bleached forest would be laden with lime leaves and white flowers. To me, the bleak forests appeared like an untouched part of the devastated world, which still had some life preserved in it. My eyes always looked through the woods and searched for lost stories. I wished everybody could stand at the same window silently after sunset and look out for lost stories from the past in the black forest.

She was not as regular as the snowfalls. But on the odd lucky days, I would catch a glimpse of her. Sometimes, I waited behind the window for her, but the wait would end with darkness taking over the day. The days were dark and cloudy. Greyish-black clouds covered the sky most of the time and the sun turned out to be a guest that rarely visited. It had been days since I had seen a sunrise.

One day, after heavy snowfall, I assumed that the black forest must have turned into a cold white forest that day; I pulled back the heavy white curtains. My wishes didn't manifest, though, but I was lucky to have been there to behold the sight that unfolded. There certainly was white powder hanging on to the tree's stems and branches but the root received the most of the snows. I wanted to capture the moment and took out my camera. As I zoomed in to take a picture, I saw a lonely figure moving and crossing the scope of my lens. I zoomed out and saw her. The girl in the black overcoat stood at the edge of the woods. I focused on her face. It felt like I was standing in one corner of the world and the longest and straightest tunnel unfolded in front of my eyes, and she stood at the other end of the tunnel. I zoomed in, and it felt like the distance between her and I had reduced, and I felt closer to her. In the dark sky, she was a silvery moon. I saw the heavy overcoat on her shoulders and a scarf that was in hues of a peacock's plumage. She had shining black eyes and soft, chubby cheeks. I tried to click her photograph, but the image was not clear and soon, she vanished behind the woods.

For the first time, I felt the real warmth of an angel in the cold black forest. With time, gradually, the unknown figure turned into an object of fascination for me. She was like a puzzle to me. The curiosity of human nature pieces together all the riddles until some clarity appears. It would not be wrong if I say that I was virtually paralyzed by her. I did not realize it then, but I was almost hypnotized by my own thoughts about her, as I spent time imagining by the window.

The Hut Across The Woods

One afternoon, I went to the reception at the hotel to collect my work-lot. It was incomplete. While collecting it, I thought there wasn't a more perfect time to ask about the woods behind the hotel. I was told that some people lived in their huts on the other side of the woods. They could not afford a wooden cottage or a concrete home. The receptionist called them refugees. I asked if I could go on for a walk through the woods. The receptionist was a little surprised at first, but agreed. He took me through the backyard. It was little muddy. Through a rusted iron-grilled door, I stepped into the cold woods. I puffed my cigarette, and felt the heavy smoke entering my cold lungs. With the camera in my other hand, I stepped carefully through mud and slippery snow. I hoped to see her again. I would at least know what she looked like in real.

What was it that was driving me then? I was not sure of. I just wanted to see her. I wanted to know more about her. There was something unknown, and something felt incomplete. There was a battle in my mind where thousands of thoughts tried to gain prominence. Puffing and panting, I crossed the woods, the dead brown leaves, the black soil and the dead logs. After I crossed the woods, I was into a different world. I was not standing on an asphalt road anymore. On the hill station, roads not often accessed were made up of concrete. There were around a dozen wooden huts covered with steel sheets for roofs. They were more like *zozo* huts, but only smaller in size. Outside the huts, there were a few tin boxes, burnt logs and clothes lines with old clothes hanging off them. A layer of snow had settled over it all. Around the hut, some wooden logs were placed. A few children played with snowballs and a few dogs lay around the ashes of the burnt wooden logs. I crossed the road. It did look like a refugee camp, but it was not one. There was peace everywhere. Water was dripping from a tap in the corner of the street. There was a pile of wooden logs, branches and twigs in front of almost each house. I saw a girl to the left, packing chopped logs inside jute bags. She wore a pair of black ankle-length boots that looked heavy. She did not pay attention to me and was busy chopping wood while her long black hair dangled from under her colorful scarf. She was not aware of my presence. I felt like I shared some kind of a bond with her and that we had known each other for long. There was a small shop on the side of the road. It was actually the patio of a house that was converted into the shop. A curtain separated the house and the shop. The mud hut was small and was meant to house two people comfortably. I stood in front of the shop. After she finished what she was doing, she looked up at me. She walked up to the counter.

"Sir! Would you like some tea?" she asked.

"Yeah," I replied.

She went to the back of the shop. I saw her go up to the clay oven. There was an old lady sitting in the corner beside a cooking platform in the front room, chopping vegetables. There were a few packets of noodles, some bread and a few vegetables lying in the corner. After offering me a chair, the girl went about her work in preparation of making tea. Soon, I was served the tea. She went to the corner seat and began chopping vegetables with the old lady. Sometimes, she smiled when she caught my eye. I sipped my tea slowly, looking around while sitting on a wooden chair. The tin-shed was bolted tightly and fastened with nuts and hooks to prevent cold air from entering. There was a loose wet tarpaulin hanging on one side. It was torn and old. From the right, I heard noises from the city. I could see the hoardings and the antennas in distant top. The woods between the hotel and the shop though were the same, yet looked different from different places. After paying for my tea, I left the hut to explore. Later, I saw her taking out the snow from the roof of the tin shed with a shovel. She looked at me and smiled and continued working, undisturbed. I lit another cigarette. She would, while working, sometimes look at me. She was struggling to move the cold and heavy shovel, but she was not incapable of doing it. Soon, she got done and came towards me.

"Did you like the tea?" she looked concerned about her business.

"Yes! I did," I said.

"Thank you," she smiled as she went inside.

We do not pay too much attention to a person while we are in their presence, but after they are gone, temporarily or permanently, we think of them. I'm no different. There, then, even if I wanted to, I did not pay much attention to her. Also, one never knows much about another until and unless they choose to reveal anything about themselves. So, I tried to find reasons to remain in her company for a little more time. I was obsessing over her in my mind. There were always windows of opportunity available to know more about her, and I didn't want to miss them at any cost. I decided that the best way for me to stay there and know more about her was to opt to eat something –though I was not hungry.

"Do you have something to eat?" I asked the old lady, while my eyes looked inside for the girl.

"Yeah, we have *momos*. Do you want some?" she asked.

"Come inside! You should not be standing out in the cold for too long!" the girl said, from inside.

That was when I realized I was standing out in the snow. I entered the patio, and stepped in through the curtain. It had two rooms in all. The front room had a bed in the corner. The second room was beyond a curtain which fluttered, giving me the chance to get a glimpse of the yellow bulb glowing inside. She had taken off her scarf. It was for the first time that I saw her as she was – without anything covering her head or face. She had shiny black eyes, reddened cheeks, a long nose, and lovely teeth. Of all her features, her eyes were the most appealing. They were dreamy, and did all the talking. Looking at those eyes, as I would do, later, it was easy to guess what she was about to say. I felt like I had known those eyes from long before, and had seen them earlier. It felt like they spoke to you whenever you looked at them. I could not take my eyes off her. Her eyes, to me, seemed like a doorway into another world. I was on earth, but I was flying a thousand miles all at once. While I was captivated by her, she was oblivious to the effect she had on me. She was busy attending to everything that needed her attention. I could hear the water boiling. Steam appeared to be filling up the room. I left the room and got back onto the portico. Her mother, I presumed that's who the old lady was, got busy with her hookah, continued sitting peacefully in the corner of the portico. The *momos* were ready, and the girl brought them to me. Sitting down quietly in one corner of the portico, I spent as much time as I could, relishing the *momos* while virtually enjoying my time with her. In the days to come, I realized that she had grown to have some sort of a power over me.

I spent almost all of my afternoons there. I went there every day for tea and lunch. I felt like a teenager, on the cusp of adulthood, but yet bereft of the innocence of childhood. For her part, she always welcomed me. I was always excited to see her. I didn't know if she waited for me or not – but she welcomed me all the same. We didn't talk much – but I did notice her gaze on me now and then. No matter how hectic it was at her shop, she always spared a look for me. It seemed like a questioning look – as though she meant to say, "So...?"

A week passed in this fashion – and though we never exchanged any more than just a few customary gazes and questioning looks, I felt a deep connection with her now, more than ever. I became familiar with the sights and sounds of the place – right from the rustic old-worldly charm to the stray dogs and kids sitting around log fires. Most times, I was the only customer for the day. Not many people liked to come out of their houses in winter, and the odd occasions when there were a lot of people, it might have had something to do with the exceptional arrival of the sun on the scene. I loved sitting around the log fire at her hut. Her mother often started the conversation with me. The girl would join in and sit across me on the other side of the log-fire. I loved the time we spent doing that. Her mother had a lot of questions for me – who I was, my job, my hobbies and interests, things I did, things I liked to do, places I'd visited, cultures I was accustomed to and such else. She looked directly into my eyes when she asked me her questions. I answered her to the best of my abilities, but sometimes, I would fumble because some questions were too queer to answer. She would smile at me – and that really energized me. I was sure that things were looking up for the better where I was concerned. She would look at me with a challenge in her eyes: as though daring me to come up with bolder and more audacious answers. On occasions, she would get up and leave the room with a mischievous smile spread on her face.

Was I lucky? No.

The kind of profession I was into was a bit of a people-magnet, and always attracted a large fan following. I had fans ranging from children to senior citizens. People tended to think I was living it up as a photographer-cum-wildlife-enthusiast – but none of them really got to see the vicissitudes of the profession, or even understand that there was a downside that came from the inherent uncertainty in the field. Mine was a life of compromise – and vindication was elusive. But the best part was the value that my work added to the lives of others – that made me feel special. She made me feel even more special than that.

With time, our bond grew out of the confines of her shop. I showed her the nuances and techniques of photography, and also sifted through a small album that I carried along with me. We spoke about a range of things: winter, Shimla before the nineties, villages in the valley, the places I had been to and our lives. I always had her full attention. She was interested in photography, culture and food. Unaware of most other things when we talked, we were almost hypnotized by the other. She would revel in contentment by vicariously living the things I told her. She loved flowing like a river, and I stood still, looking at her like I was a sailor charting new waters. She didn't care one bit about what she came across as – it was always natural, and she had no trouble being and expressing herself as she was. She was like a dream. She was deceptive in her demeanor. She looked calm, but contained within herself was something ethereal that came forth through her eyes. A dream that she had lived, carefully nestled below her wings. She just needed a sky that she could fly across, and wind beneath her wings to help her float through. I could sense it from her inquisitiveness, amazement and sense of surprise at my responses to her questions.

"Do you know what figs are?" she asked me one day.

"Yes," I said. We had not opened up to each other as much just yet, but we had achieved a certain unspoken level of comfort.

"How do you know about it?" she asked.

"Well, I have tasted fig juice," I said.

"Okay. But, that does not mean that you know what a fig is like," She continued. "Liking something is different from knowing what it is." I loved her candor and her wisdom. She was definitely right.

"Ha-ha! Yes, I suppose that is true. Then, as you rightly say, I do not know what a fig is!" I said.

"Tomorrow, I am going to cook green fig curry. If you would like to come over to try it, you should!" That was an indirect invitation from her.

"Okay. So that's why you asked me this?" I asked.

"Yes indeed!" She said, smiling.

We enjoyed our walk through the woods. I loved being with her in the confines of the woods. Perhaps I wanted to keep our relationship – or whatever this was – under wraps, for the world judges everything it sees. Was that my care for her reputation or was it over-protectiveness?

Later, I learned her heart beat for me as much as mine did, for her. Life went on at its pace – the two of us spent time in each other's presence, stealing glances surreptitiously, conscious of each other's presence and our feelings for the other. On the surface of it all, we were just two random people in public view. We were trying to fit into the life with a harmonious resonance. I looked at her from the corner of my eye. I noticed that she was doing the same. We were aware of the existence, and that we had some kind of consciousness pivoted towards each other. We reciprocated only in gestures. On the face of it, we acted like nothing happened. We had our own codes yet unrevealed to each other. We were aware that there was something going on between us – and we didn't want to give it a name just yet. We were acting sly to each other and to the society.

I felt like I was going to have lunch with people who shared some attributes with me, but for the most part, were really anonymous to me. I had been to some lunches where a lot of cutlery confused me. People judged my every gesture and the cunning eyes followed false handshakes and fake compliments that seldom came from the heart. I did not have too many choices where my clothes went. I had a few rugged, out-door terrain clothing with me, and I couldn't choose among the lot. I was not able to decide which one to choose from, and I tried my best to look soft in my rugged clothes. I don't know what degree of soberness that my rough cargo pants or my three layered jacket gave me. Nonetheless, undeniably, I felt special. Wearing my heavy boots, I walked through the woods, and soon, I was standing before the mud hut.

She was already waiting for me. I could see her from a distance. There was no familiar black overcoat slung over her shoulders this time. She was dressed in a blue jacket made out of a silky material, with tufts of fur hanging from the sleeves and around the neck. She had the peacock-blue scarf around her head. I loved that scarf. It is these little things that add to the beauty of a person. She smiled at me when she saw me. I loved her smile – her soft pink lips framed a beautiful set of teeth.

"You are late!" she said with her one eyebrow raised and a mischievous smile scattered over her lips. I guess she loved teasing me at times.

"Yeah, I had to find the receptionist so he could open the backyard gate and..." I was cut in between before I could finish my sentence.

"So, the lunchtime guest appears out of the forests again, huh?" She cut me in between.

"Yeah, because I love these woods," I nodded and said.

"And yet you got late! You could have asked the receptionist what street to take to get here," she said, her eyes reflecting her shrewdness.

I had a lot of thoughts in my mind about how a stranger should behave. But to me, the person standing seven feet away was not a stranger any more. An uncommon, yet the warmth with which she had given me an unusual welcome, made me forget all my little sophistications which I had been carrying along from my hotel room till the hut. She had no place for judgment in her heart.

Seeing me lost in thought, she said, "Oh yeah! I forgot that you are an adventurer who loves wood!" She laughed at her joke and I could not contain my smile.

"Come on inside! Here is your chair," she said, beckoning me into the shop.

The arrangement that day was different. That place always struck me as being one of its kinds. There was no sophistry to it, and nothing pretentious – but it had such a beautiful and quaint feel to it. The reason why loved the place was undoubtedly her – but what also made it so precious was the sanctity attached to the peaceful solitude. I hated rich parties. Everything from the fine china wares to the crowds, to the constant need to remain prim and proper so as not to offend anyone – was absolutely repulsive. I've always believed that humanity grows only when the hearts communicate, and not when there is an idle pursuit of purported sophistry. This is why I enjoy simplicity. The greatest people are always simple, and the richer and more flamboyant ones are often really empty vessels. Standing inside that hut at the moment, with her by my side, and the beautiful landscape surrounding us, it hit me how valuable that precious moment was. We had no need to pretend.

By the time I settled down in my chair, she had gone inside. Sometimes, I got more than I asked for. It was a moment of authenticity – a moment when I could not lie to myself, a moment when I could not pretend, a moment when I was not going to be judged. It was no different from lying before a campfire with strangers I just met while hiking in the morning. No one judged anyone. Everyone fell from the sky holding hands. When the parachutes opened, we were scattered in different directions, within moments.

I noticed a mud-Chula in the corner of the patio. Smoky smudges had found themselves on the wall near the Chula, with a couple of wooden logs and a wind pipe lying askew on the ground. A few utensils were piled one over the other, gleaming in the bleak light. In another corner, there was a wooden cot with a pile of bedding on it. A rather heavy quilt was folded neatly and kept towards the head of the cot. An old printed bed-sheet hung down from the mattress on the cot. Everything looked old and worn, but was still clean. Above the bedding, there was a large mosquito-net tied to assorted things higher up on different walls to stay hung up. A jute rope hung across the room and a few clothes were laid out to dry on the make-shift clothes-line. What I liked the most about this setting was the spiritual solace it offered. The song of silence was punctuated by the whistling of the low winds. It was the kind of a place where your heart could wander a thousand miles while you stayed in the same place. Smoke must have blackened the steel sheet and the thatched roof, as patches of black were seen in the make-shift ceiling. An old and rusted lantern hung over the mud-Chula. Bamboos were used to support the hut, and ran the breadth of the room. She had arranged the same wooden table that they used to serve tea to their customers, for me. She came out smiling.

"Is your shop not open today?" I asked, "And where is your mother?"

"She has gone to the flea market in the lower bazaar today, because it's a Sunday and we do not open for business on Sundays," she said while putting the green fig curry on the table.

"So, here it is. There are chapattis in the box. I think you will enjoy the meal," she was arranging my meal over the table.

She set the table, placing a glass of water to the right of the plate. She began serving me. I looked at her hand – the white, pale hand reminded me of the hands of a newly married bride. She had red polish on her nails and wore a few golden bangles.

After she was done serving me, she looked up at me and stood aside. I looked up at her and we smiled. I was nervous. I tried to look at her in the face again, but I could not raise my eyes above her waist. I decided to go ahead and eat. The fig curry was spicy and sweet, all at once. I ate quietly.

She broke the silence and asked, "Do you like it?"

"Yes! This is really tasty," I said, eating silently.

I did not know how to keep the conversation alive. I knew I'd become good friend with her – and there was a strong connection, but there was also something invisible that kept us apart. It was very hard to figure out how to bridge the unseen and unknown gap. There was something hindering the flow of the river, but it was obscure and we couldn't understand it. Knowing the unknown was like hunting for something which I had not seen yet.

While eating, I made up my mind and decided not to lose any more of the time that we had in each other's company, and decided to take the plunge by talking to her candidly.

"Please sit. You should not be standing," I said.

"Nah, its fine," she said.

"I would enjoy my meal better if you sit," I insisted.

"Okay," she said, and sat down.

"So how many people are there in your family?" I wanted to keep the conversation afloat.

"Only my mother, my younger brother and me. My brother studies at a boarding in Solan. Shimla is more expensive for education. My mother and I live and work here. She runs the shop and I take tuitions. I completed my B.Ed. this year and am still waiting for an appointment letter to join a school here in Shimla. I love teaching. My father was a soldier and he died in a war fifteen years ago when I was still a child. I think I was in class six or seven then. We got some compensation from the government, but it was not sufficient," she finished.

I looked straight into her eyes when she finished. While talking, her eyes were fixed on my spoon, as it moved from the plate to my mouth and back. I looked straight into her eyes. When our eyes met, we felt a buzz. But we pretended like there was no one around to steal our gaze, and everything was normal. I felt the blood rushing through my veins at breakneck speed. I managed a weak smile.

"So, how many places do you know in Shimla now?" she had not much left to talk about her family.

"Well, I have been to almost all the places inside the city, and even a few outside the city," I said.

"How do you like Shimla then?" she asked.

"It was one of my many dreams to capture the white world, and that's why I am here in winter" I replied.

Like a child, she continued asking questions about Shimla and the things I liked about it.

"I know some places where you might enjoy photography but they are little away from the city. You will have to walk a lot to get there. Moreover, we cannot go there at any time. It should be the morning or evening," she said.

"You must have photographed some golden peaks, I'm sure! Do you want to photograph the valley and a vast field of snow which changes color with the sunset? It's called sunset point," she asked me.

"Oh! Yes! Can we go there?" I asked.

"Yes, we can. Finish your lunch and we leave then?" she asked.

"Yes, let's go. I will have to get my tripod and lenses!" I said.

I quickly finished my lunch and almost ran to the hotel. I wanted to be with her. I was also feeling lucky to have been invited. On top of that, I felt luckier because she was going to accompany me.

"Meet me near the Gurudwara which is to the right of your hotel. I will wait for you there. Don't follow the woods this time again," she called after me and chuckled.

Golden Apples

I picked up my things from the hotel. I wasn't really that concerned about the photographs – the truth was that I wanted to spend time with her. I trudged out to the Gurudwara to meet her, as she had instructed.

"Okay! So, we take the route by that pavement. It is a little lonely, but we can reach fast. People go there in spring because you can see the valley, blue skies and green trees. In winters, the snow changes color with the sunset and its looks very beautiful," She gesticulated like a child when I returned with my photography kit.

We walked on as she decided, talking animatedly about what we were about to see and photography and the like.

We finally reached the spot. It was a little windy, and was perched a little higher than the rest of the town. Below us there was a big field of snow that lay untouched. It spread across the breadth of the valley, and stretched on for miles. A vast unending stretch of white lay before us. Beyond the world of white, there stood a valley and series of shining peaks.

"You cannot dip your leg in the river for more than thirty seconds. The river directly descends from the Himalayas," she said as she pointed to a river flowing along the valley.

I was still speechless after seeing the idyllic setting before me. I looked at the river. The river had frozen over with the snow – with streaks of white punctuating an otherwise glazed surface. It looked as though there was a wet blue canvas and a painter was continuously painting shades of silver with a brush. If the wet canvas was shaken, shades of silver would have disappeared. With another shake, they would have reappeared momentarily. When the wind nudges flowing water and tips it to the perfect angle where the sun catches in the icy ripples, it glints in the air with an ardent force of reflection. The icy river caught rays from the sun and let them glint out into open air. I saw exuberance engulfing her little face. She was talking away as usual. I clicked a few photographs for myself, and just to see her happiness grow by leaps and bounds, I kept clicking. It was time for sunset. The snow became a spectacular sight, changing colors with the descent of the sun. With the changing phases and colors, the snowy visuals were taking a thousand different colors at different places. It was a display of fireworks rolling out on the cold snow.

Whole of the valley was covered with snow. The horizon was hazy with the mists. A thin edged winter-line was shining clearly though. There were chunks of dark clouds hanging in the bright colorful sky everywhere. Where the sun was setting behind the hills at the horizon, was shining brightly. Soft edges of chunk of clouds suspending in the foreground were burning under the halo of the setting sun. Clouds suspending away were in disguise with the dim lit sky.

Far across the river, fields, villages, hills- all were covered with the snow. Hedgy dykes of the fields and countryside streets looked like lines of a maze cropping up out of the frozen world. Patches of pine trees over the hills and small huts of the villages were the only visible objects on the earth.

It had become harder for me to decide where to start the photography from. Every photo-shoot scope had a thousand scopes with in. I had little time to play around with the firework rolled out on the cold snow field. I was overwhelmed by the beauty blossomed in front of my eyes. I wanted to do random clicking vehemently with little time left in my hand. I was doing so too- focus and click. I did not how many pictures was I able to shoot with little time left in my hand.

Later, as we left, we walked together, rubbing shoulders and nudging each other's arms. We spent some time looking at the pictures I had taken.

"Look at this one," I said trying to show her a few of the photographs.

"Wait, wait, wait! Don't change! I want to see!" she said. She sifted through the photographs, paused at whichever ones attracted her most.

"This one looks so pretty, no?" She looked at my face, waiting to see me approve.

She waited until I nodded, looking at me eagerly. We would catch each other's eye and laugh. I don't know why we laughed – but those moments when we did, was delightful. She showed me around – we saw different places, especially where the flea market was being held.

"See, golden apples!" she clutched my right arm as she pointed to a bunch of golden apples displayed at the front of a shop.

"I thought you wanted to shoot them. So...," she stopped.

I looked at her and smiled. She looked a little shy and childish at the same time. She looked at me like an innocent child, as though she had tried to express an innocent message with her compelling eyes. She also smiled at me in return. Whenever she smiled, her cheeks bloomed red and its radiance lit up every corner of her face as if the sun had descended down from the sky and made her face its home. It fit perfectly in line with the bang which peeked out from under the round white fur cap she wore.

The next moment, she realized that she had held onto my right arm. She was still exuberant with the feelings from the valley. She unclutched her grip. We walked together, thinking of the time we had spent together over the past hour.

Unconscious behavior is sometimes a result of repressed feelings. They lie underneath and stay hidden, coming forth in expression out of nowhere, all of a sudden. We had fallen back on earth from our sojourn in the clouds. All the merriment, elation and delight were lost in the air. The rapture created an hour ago faded away in the cold air around. I personally found that unacceptable when we had to over conduct ourselves within the social norms. Of course, I felt sad because we had to drop away the exaltation within the social norms.

We saw the Gurudwara that we had both met at. She had to take a left turn - and I tried to tell her that I wanted to spend more time with her. But, my throat denied any support for speech. I wished I could hold and rub her hands, but I had missed the opportunity to do that. We were back where we started.

"Thanks for accompanying me! I have to leave for my room," I said.

"Yeah! I also need to go home, my mom must be waiting for me," she understood what I was trying to say within the words.

We parted ways for the day. Before stepping inside the hotel, I couldn't resist myself, and so I turned around to get a glimpse of her. The snow-filled street shone golden under the yellow street lights. A lonely figure walked silently, dressed in a blue jacket with fur around the collars and sleeves. I wished she would turn around and take a look at me. I waited but she did not. I stepped inside the hotel. When I was inside my room, I stood next to my window. There was silence in the air. Fog skimmed under the yellow street lights and cold waves washed my eyes. I lit up a cigarette. I smoked a few puffs and gazed out into the dark. I felt like she was looking at me from the beyond the woods.

Melancholy in the Cold Woods

The next day, all my work lot had arrived. It was a sweet surprise. My missing camera set, my list of contacts and places to be covered and some personal favorite items were packed inside safely. I loved the letter that assigned a four-by-four Gypsy for me, with a driver, to travel about in. The Gypsy arrived soon after, and the driver was called Raam Singh. I learned later that he was from Kashmir originally, but had relocated to Himachal where his family lived. He was middle-aged, perhaps between thirty-five to forty years. He was well built and had contemplative eyes. He was almost half a foot taller than I was. He wore an olive-green turban and a Nehru-cut black jacket with a black kurta. Later, I would learn that he always had cigarettes and a matchbox in his pocket.

"Are you from Shimla, *Bhaiya*?" I asked him.

"*Jee saab jee*, from Chhota Shimla," he replied.

"Is the vehicle in good condition?" I just wanted to make sure that the vehicle was in working condition.

"*Jee saab jee*, it is old but it is in good condition. I take foreigners around on tours in this vehicle," He looked proud of his old yet strong vehicle.

The Gypsy had an open roof. It was white in color. I showed him the map and pointed out the routes I wanted to travel. With the work lot in my stride, I had everything I needed, and I was now ready to travel and shoot photos. I was eager to find locations that I could photograph. Raam Singh was a great companion – he took me about the place, showed me landmarks and nature's own marvels in the region. I was ready to drive through the hills and the circuitous roads. I felt like a child left at a candy shop, unable to choose from hundreds of candies. We were exploring locations for the photo-shoot in the outskirts of Shimla. We drove for miles through the valley. The chances of finding a good location for the shoot seemed slim. One needed to have a good sense of perception of the mountains. I felt like I was exploring the labyrinth of a white world. In parts, we drove along unknown valleys, following muddy and slippery trails. The harsh winter had gotten to everything. The partially frozen waters, the dark greyish-auburn collared twigs and branches lying along the street and the silence were all surely signs that the places were visited very rarely. The pine trees kept me reminding of the Christmas thought.

On the way, Raam Singh told me, "Saab jee, if we are lucky, we might see a Himalayan panther as well."

For a moment, I was scared. We were still running along the trails of the Himalayan reserve forests. We had left the villages far behind. The steepness of the road increased slowly. I felt that driving in an open vehicle in the harsh winter was absurd, but it was an offbeat part of the adventure. There was no alternative available.

No shrubs or bushes had been able to retain their leaves. There were only lonely wet branches, reddish black in color, sniffing out of the snow. Also, there were some lonely leaves lying along the roadside; soaked and left to rot or to get preserved, under the cold. Those were dark brown in color. Most of them were both wet and soaked in the melting ice or resting peacefully preserved under a layer of snow. No trees wore leaves. We drove more along the single meandering roads bargaining our chances. There was a huge silent melancholy absorbed under the snow. It was not only the water which had soaked the huge stems of the trees but also they were soaked up by a layer of melancholy hidden beneath the dark scaly barks. That was the sad part about the Jungle. In spring, the same forest would become so thick and green that looking beyond feet should become tougher. The trails looked decisive. They hid depth under the shallow snow covering them. Engine roared; wheels spun and threw away the chunks of mud, it was that hard to move ahead sometimes. Forest check-points were deserted. Wooden houses housed no one. Mild sun rays faded away midway in the sky. Our Gypsy slipped, skidded, and its tires screeched on many occasions. Going through hedges and oaks did not always land us at the highest or at any perfect picturesque point. We always ended up at some point in the woods from where the trail would thin down. We would drive back and find some another route with greater expectations. There was no one to talk to except Raam singh. Puffing smokes along the higher ranges in deep winter was of course a different experience then.

I remember, when we crossed the village, there were only a few people sitting around the fire. As we crossed the space, people turned to look at us like we were crazy aliens. We stopped on occasion to smoke and get warm before some of these fires. But it was still a tiring journey.

For a person who found solace in nature, driving miles along the deserted cold valleys should substantiate Maslow's theory of self-actualization. I was no exception. Hours of cold wind and silence, gave me time to think again about someone who was always on my mind. When we were driving through, one with nature, I did not miss her at all. But, there were special moments when I missed her a lot. I was not a good pattern-reckoner, but there was something extraordinary in each of those moments when I thought of her: when I looked far ahead at the chain of mountains; when I drank hot tea in a remote village; when I was crossing some appealing places which were way overly beautiful.

Was there a pattern? There was no precise answer. I could not articulate that. I felt her presence when I was alone and had time to appreciate the beauty of nature. Maybe I needed someone to appreciate and show me beauty through different eyes. When it was too cold, I needed someone to share tea with and stand beside me. I arrived at a conclusion, then, that it was the aesthetic beauty that when came into the scene, I needed her to show me the world.

Silence Does the Talking

I could not deny that I had begun to like her. I chanced upon something rare in my relationship with her. I was a little wary of asking her out because I was worried it might disturb the harmony of our friendship. I was not an outgoing person by nature, and to ask a woman out for a date was neither easy for me. On top of that, the incident with the "Golden apples" had drawn a line of control between us. Moreover, I could not take some time out for her with my work lot arrived lately.

I believed in miracles, though, and I also knew that I had to be vigilant about watching out for miracles – they didn't just happen all the time. Once or twice, I saw her in the market, but could not gather the courage to step closer to her. I didn't know if she was aware of me, but I wished she would turn around and our eyes would meet and that we would smile at each other. But this way, I was making up my own coliseum and needed to come out of it. I had to approach her before it was too late. I had to win her over. I think I had misinterpreted everything about the "Golden apples" incident. When people say that we should not assume things, they are probably right. Different minds interpret the same thing differently.

One day, I decided I would just ask her to join me on a ride. I drove up to her house. She was busy with a hose in her little garden.

"Hey! What's up?" she looked at me smiling when I parked the Gypsy in front of her house.

"I was planning to check out some of the places around here for some possible photographs. Want to come along and help me?" I asked her.

"Not now, can we go in the afternoon? I need to buy some things for my household needs now," she said.

"Sure," it took me a while to go back to the hotel.

I was sure then that she had no issues about hanging out with me. I asked the driver to stay back at the hotel and be in touch in case I would need his help. Hundreds of thoughts haunted my mind. It was not easy to get rid of them. I wanted to silence my screaming thoughts and just drive on until I would see her. But this is what happens when you care too much about these things.

Possessiveness creeps into the picture, and encourages presumption. I went back to her place in the afternoon.

"Coming?" I shouted out.

"Yeah, I am coming. I thought you would come just after lunch. I had no work to do, so I was knitting a scarf for my mother. She loves purple," she said as she came out of the hut.

"Where do you want to go?" she asked.

"I have no idea. Tell me where I should go to find the best places to take photographs. Take me to the horizon and the farthest place on this planet," I raised my hands trying to accommodate the whole horizon in my arm's length. I was excited.

"Ha ha! Okay. Let's go to another beautiful place," she replied.

"Hop in. So, where are we going?" I asked her.

"You asked for the farthest place! Let's go to the lower valleys then," she was prankish.

Sitting with her in the Gypsy was a smashing experience. I could not look at her for long, but the rear view mirror helped me.

"You know what?" she asked, raising her voice as she came close to my left ear.

"A lot of couples go there in the summer or in spring! But no one dares to go there in the winter. It's so dangerously cold! If you go deeper along the river, it gets even more beautiful!"

We were silent for some time.

"Believe me," she reconfirmed that she was talking to me.

Sometimes, I hated being moody. I knew I was a hypersensitive person and it took no time for hyper-anxiety to take me over. Even if I knew that I could breathe out the tensions and take control over peace of my mind, I still could not do that because I simply felt helpless. That was more like I was knowingly committing the mistakes even if I had not wanted to.

So I didn't respond to her talks because I was being hypersensitive about what had happened into the past. There was a long silence. My eyes were on the road and my ears were focused on the sound of the engine. Silence had enveloped us.

She looked happy, but composed. I always imagined her as a playful heart in my mind. I never imagined that she would be such an inquisitive girl. That was a different side of her. I had read somewhere that it were the people who talked a lot had a lot to say. We always try to be, whatever we most long to be.

I cleared my throat to grab her attention but she kept looking out of the window. I cleared my throat again.

"Are you okay?" she turned to look at me.

"Yeah! I am fine. Where in the lower valley are we going to?" I wanted to keep the conversation alive.

"There is a road that goes down to the river. It is a very nice place for photographers and bird watchers. In winter, though, no birds can be seen except for a few Himalayan birds," she explained

"Okay," I affirmed.

"You will see where to take a turn, it will be written on a blue colored board," she said.

"Okay," I affirmed again.

I was responsible for throwing the moments I had with her to silence. We slipped into an awkward sense of quietness. Even if I wanted to talk, there was either nothing I could find in me to say, or, I would have something holding me back. She was a silent person too. If she wanted to get my attention, she would look at me until I turned around to acknowledge her. She communicated through her eyes most often – but I was not all that great at reading her eyes.

"*Niam....!.*" she said, using my name for the first time.

I looked at her. Her silent eyes looked back at me. I felt so connected with her in that moment. Her eyes never lied –

there was something so truthful about her. Every time I looked at her, it felt like the world would stop. I also always sensed some kind of pain in her heart – it was like there was a lot of unsolved emotional pain within her.

"Hmmm…" I said.

I couldn't bring myself to say anything more than that. I was still waiting for the moment to come. I was going to see another bout from her suppressed and Delphian side. We were still sitting inside. After a while she looked emotional too.

"I always wanted to go to some lonely places. I don't know why they always tended to be attractive for me. I never imagined that I would be going to one of these beautiful spots along with you," she said as I parked the vehicle.

Someday, when I would sit around with my German friends and share this part of the story with them, they might tell me that she needed someone to save her.

I let the thought pass and said, "Let's sit inside for some time."

"You don't want to photograph the river?" she asked.

"No, it's cold out there. I can photograph them tomorrow or some other day," I said.

"Okay," she said silently and looked at me.

"Tell me more," I said.

I had no idea what I wanted to hear her say, but I wanted to listen to her talking. I did not know where I gathered the courage from – but I felt like I was her savior and that she could pour her heart out to me.

"I was a shy child. I was poor in studies. I could not make many friends in my life. Though I had some, they were never permanent. They always left me," and, she switched over to something else.

"I wanted to go somewhere far away - a place that was not lesser than paradise. Sometimes, I found myself sitting beside a blue lake and getting lost in thought. I would also see an imaginary and a handsome man with me," she said, turning to look at me.

I did not know how to respond. She smiled at me; it was a shadow of a smile before she continued...

"I sometimes saw him standing on the shores of a beach with crystalline turquoise waves lashing against his feet and his long hair moving along the wind. He prefers to keep calm most of the times and let his mystical eyes do the talking. His silence gives meaning to our existence and to each other's presence." She held my hand without looking into my eyes.

"Now we are here. I did not know that I would come with someone, a complete stranger, to this place. It's as though you have been waiting for a miracle and dreaming of it for years, but when it happens, you don't trust yourself because, it's a surprise that it actually did happen! Initially, it takes you by storm, but as time passes, it begins to feel normal. Right now, I am sitting with you. I had dreamed of this very thing and it was surprising at first, the way it happened. But now that i can see it happening for real, it looks so normal! Maybe it is because I feel comfortable with you," and she got down. I followed her.

She stood beside me. She looked into my eyes when I looked down at her. I wanted her to feel free with me, and to be close to me. I gently moved her head onto my shoulder – and she didn't resist. She looked up into my eyes. I loved it most when she wrapped her arms around my arm. She would smile at me with her wide smile, and her innocent eyes would turn bigger.

"I loved it when my father would make me sit on his broad shoulders and take me to the ice-cream shop in summer. I loved looking at the stars in the night sky when I sat on his shoulders. I used to ask a lot of questions about imaginary shapes I saw up in the galaxy. My father would laugh. Maybe my questions were innocent then. We would walk through crowded streets, but, I always felt protected sitting on his shoulders. Years have passed but two things which I still carry with me are my dad's protection and the thoughts of the beautiful figures in the night sky. I imagined the same kind of protection from the imaginary guy in my dreams – but I can't decipher any more than that," she said.

"Do you feel protected when you are with me?" I asked.

"When I close my eyes and hold you tight, I feel that everything I have always dreamed of has come true. But when I open my eyes, I find myself in the same world and it gets harder for me to compare between both, my dreams and the present. That's why I close my eyes while talking to you and holding your arms. But I never thought I would meet an adventurer and a free soul like you, someday."

"Come here," I said and pulled her closer. She squeezed herself up to me.

"I don't know who drives the universe and who drives my emotions, but I will say that you are a nice guy," she said.

"I want to know more about you," I said.

"Why?" she asked.

"I don't know. I just want to listen to you talk," I replied.

"In my childhood, I saw different facets of society. How people turn away from others and such other things. I was never a bright student at school. I failed thrice in a row in class four. My friends never treated me differently though. It was their parents who would brainwash them about not hanging out with students who were dull. Those were terrible days. I felt so let down by myself. I lacked confidence. I had no courage to go forward and ask my teacher for permission to use the restroom; I preferred the backseat. I was so scared and insecure that I was afraid of what might happen next. I was mocked and cried alone. It was a routine," she said with trembling voice.

"Are you crying?" I looked into her eyes.

She did not seem to care for my question and kept talking-

"Everyone moved to different classes, but I was still sitting in the same place with the same old books. Do you know how it feels to lose a set of friends and when juniors call you "*Didi*" out of respect? Do you know how it feels to face your neighbors who regard you a poor kid? I was afraid to go out. Now I realize why I like to be with my mother. My family and a few friends were by my side. I was unfortunate to have lost my friends over the years. Now I understand why I love giving tuitions to children"

"Yeah, I suppose you search for your lost childhood there. You might not have found friendship as a child, but now, you are mature enough to do so much good for the world," I said.

A man tends to pursue what he missed in his life. Maybe that's why parents relate their own examples to their children, and try to ensure that their children don't make the same mistakes that they themselves did.

"One day, my father went to the principal in school to ask why I failed. She could not reply convincingly. My father paid to admit me into another school to help me make up for all the years I did not pass," she said.

Different people see different things in the same person. In scientific terms, the process of evaluating someone is like finding the maximum likelihood. It's like drawing up a result in pursuit of the hidden variables. But I don't do that. I prefer to know a person from a more anthropological perspective. Human beings are all the same, but it's the cultural, a socio-economic background that makes the difference. I just see a good heart in everyone and I don't want to miss the goodness in everyone. I read somewhere that when someone was in love his artistic senses touch new heights.

I could not resist myself, and asked her, "What makes you feel that I am a nice guy?"

"You love nature. A person who loves nature can't be bad at heart."

I smiled.

"You are a little spiritual, too, because you are close to nature."

I smiled again. The sun was going to set soon. With the changing colors of the evening sky, the color of the water began changing. With her watching me in comfortable silence, I picked out my camera. She took care of the tripod and we moved onto fixing the pods. I took many photos of the landscape. Sometimes, she lingered around me while I focused to take a shot. When I looked at her, she smiled at me in return. When I was done with a shot she savored, she ran up to me to ask if she could see the photo. We would then surf through a lot of pictures.

"Do you remember when you told me that I can't handle the cold on my feet for more than thirty seconds?" I was talking about the river descending down from Himalayas

"Yeah, I do. Want to try doing it? Come on! Let's try it!" She was too quick.

I felt helpless. She was really dynamic. In minutes, she had already made her way to the river. We took off our shoes and walked along the boulders up to the river. Our feet grew colder.

"*Oh my God!*" she shouted, gripping my jacket.

"My feet are too cold," I held her.

We dared not to put our feet inside the water. After a while, I asked her, "Have you ever photographed the plain evening sky?"

"Yeah, I have tried to. I could not capture it well! "

"I am going to try it," I wanted her to show my skills.

We moved away a good distance from the river to find a spot. I decided to lie down on the white sand under the tripod.

"You want to look through the lenses?" I wanted to touch her and wanted her to come closer to me.

"Yeah," she crawled over me as I moved away from under the tripod.

"Be careful. Go on, click a few photos," I offered my arms as a support to her and laid beside her.

"The ground is cold," she said, and rested her head on my arm.

She tried to focus and adjust the lenses. I suddenly felt a wave of sadness that a time could come when I would miss her. Meanwhile, she looked through the lens and tried clicking a few pictures. I looked at her sideways. I felt insecure – I knew how much I would miss her. I wanted to rest quietly with her, while she would look up and shoot pictures of the sky. I wondered if she felt what I was feeling, and if she would miss me as much as I would miss her. I did feel that there were some vibes we exchanged. The valleys that once echoed our laughter now seemed silent again. The sky seemed to recapitulate the same story with a sad, crimson sunset. Soon, darkness would dethrone the evening skies and the sullen winter night would be back.

"Are you okay?" she asked.

"Widen the curvature of the lenses, you can capture the curvature of the sky this way," I told ignoring her question.

She made some adjustments but was quick to look at me again.

"No. You are thinking of something!" she insisted.

"No, nothing of that sort," I replied and smiled as well. She fixed her caring gaze over me for some time and then turned towards the lenses.

The sun was soon going to set down. The sky seemed to mourn the loss of the crimson saturation. I felt numb. Her eyes were shut now, and she laid on her back, facing the sky. I was reading the contours of her face. She had a flat forehead. There were a few water droplets clinging to her eye-lids. I looked at her for a little more time. I closed my eyes, and spent some time listening to her breathing. I opened my eyes to look at her again – she was still in the same position. I closed my eyes again. Stealthily, I moved my fingers close to her left hand. There was a spark when my hands touched hers. My breath caught in my throat. I left my fingers beside her hand, a practiced casual flair to achieve a state of unintentional action. Our fingers gently brushed each other's, and suddenly, she held on tight. Slowly, I felt her grip closing over my fingers.

"*Niam…!*" she said.

"Hmmm…"

"It's getting dark. We should leave now," she said.

I got up and helped her getting up. We walked to the Gypsy. There was no talking. She held onto my right arm. We sat inside and I turned on the engine. It had now turned very cold. While I drove, she leaned on my left shoulder with her eyes closed. After crossing my hotel, I asked her if I could drive little slower until her home. By the time we reached her house, snowflakes had started falling from the sky. Under the yellow high street lights and in front of the vehicle's main light, they would turn into golden flecks floating lazily on the air. I could not save much time and we arrived in front of her house. I pressed the brakes. She got down silently, smiling as though she was again asking me if I wanted to just let her go. Just as she turned to leave, I reached out and held her hand. She was not surprised.

"I want to hug you," that was more like asking her consent.

"Okay!"

I got down and she came closer to me. I opened out my arms and she fit perfectly into them. I rubbed her back for a moment. We looked at each other and hugged again.

"I'll go now?" she asked.

"Goodnight. Take care," I replied.

She stood at her door, until I drove ahead and took a turn.

Living Portraits of Shimla

I did not want to give her false hopes. Some precious gems are supposed to be cherished, and are not to be worn. She was among the ones you admire from a distance. I did not want her to expect something out of me that I could not deliver. Most relationships in the world are built on certain conditions. The reputation of being a wanderlust that I carried was conditional in its inherent nature. Most friends that I made were born out of conditions or reasons. My relationship with her was unconditional and had come out of nowhere. There were probably planetary movements in our favor, or luck had indeed found a place. We had met, and it all just happened the way it did. Some things have their own rules, things that define their existence. One doesn't question their validity. My relationship with her was one of those things.

We should not name an unsaid relationship. By naming it, we draw a picture which defines it. I had no idea what we were in reality – were we friends or more? Or were we parallel lines walking separate paths that would never cross?

With her, there was only one thing on my mind- I would never hurt her because she had enough of hurting. It had already been more than a month since I was there. Glancing through the dated pages of my diary made me realize how long I had already been there for. I loved the winter there. I liked it when cold winds left my nose red. I liked playing with snowballs with kids there. After she came into the picture, I considered that my luckiest winter.

Sometimes I wondered what kind of unknown world I had gotten into. I met her and we shared our space and time together. Why could I not enjoy with her without brooding over the present? People often told me to live in the present. But I couldn't – my mind was always thinking about the uncertain future. When one has been hurt by his past, he is often in search of the truth. Why couldn't I hold onto the pleasant things in my past? Where was I lacking? Was I a different person back then? I had turned into an intuitive person over time, certainly. A bad past had created repentance and confusion in me – and I began seeing my past as a personal failure. I wanted to learn from my past, and avoid confusion since I wanted self-actualization. The more I wanted to learn from my mistakes, the more I would have to face my doubts in the face. With her, I hated my inquisitiveness, for the resultant effect was confusion and impatience on my part. Why was I trying to find the truth so desperately? Why did all these beautiful journeys finish? Everything annoyed me.

Gradually, almost all my navigators got to know of her. Besides navigators, the guys at the hotel and a few shopkeepers in the market with whom I had developed good friendships were aware of our relationship. They were respectful of us.

Her shop was situated at what I would call a vantage point. Behind the huts, there began a trail going down into the valley. The valley was home to many natives who climbed up the hill to reach Shimla every day for their bread and butter. Shimla was still run by the natives. Be it the porters who carried loads through narrow circuitous strips, or the rickshaw pullers who ferried visitors to places around, or the guides, milkmen, drivers running the local buses and taxis, fruit sellers and vegetable sellers - they were all natives. It was hard for anyone else to do their jobs – and yet, they thrived comfortably on the meager amounts they made. They walked a distance of two to three miles to come to Shimla for work every day.

On days when I used to return early from my assignment, I went straight to her shop. It was a different life altogether, there. I considered myself lucky to have found that spot. Their lives and nature always inspired me. I wanted to visit their homes at least once. In the evening, her shop was flooded with the locals. They had deep, contemplative eyes, but innocent and honest faces. They were often dressed in long overcoats. They had tough physiques, but soft hearts. They respected me. Seeing me photograph things around them, they were always intrigued. When I focused my lens on their rugged faces, they did not know how to pose – so I got the most natural expressions. I was always given a wooden chair to sit on. With time, others did come to the shop, and would stay longer. The others sat on benches and on the ground. Mostly, older people sat on benches, the youth sat outside the hut to smoke, and children scurried about to see the photographs. They enjoyed listening to the stories of my travels as much as I enjoyed sharing with them. I felt lucky. She eventually had to buy a Kerosene stove to meet the demands of the crowds in the evenings. Sometimes, some of the locals would call me to their houses for dinner or tea. If it was a family gathering, I always asked for her and her mother to come along – though she did come, her mother did not accompany us more than twice. I remember how nervous she used to get, while sitting amid rich people and eating with us. She was mostly silent and looked at our faces and listened to our talks. She used to get bored, but never showed it.

Once, an old man and his wife invited us. They sent an old car to receive us. The car was an old model, of a vintage kind. It had huge, flat and cushy seats which reminded me of the car in a Tom Hanks movie, "Road to Perdition". It was a beautiful experience to sit inside a vintage car. It felt royal: the big doors, the flat and clean glass, the plush cushions and the ambience it created. Inside the car, I could not control myself and I held her hand. We looked at each other smiling. I wanted to laugh out loud out of happiness. I wanted to shout. I wanted to hug her and kiss her smooth neck. I slung my hand around her waist.

It was a rainy day. The pitter-patter of the rain added more to the ambience. I felt like we were driving through the old streets of London. People walked in the rain with black umbrellas held overhead. The wet market was bathed in watery yellow light. She tried to run her fingers along the trails left behind by the water droplets on the other side of the window. The glass was cold. A light exhale against the glass made it hazy. Before the frozen puff vanished, we wrote our names on the cold glasses.

The car entered a house with a big iron gate, and drove up to a big mansion. Two men came up to the car when it stopped at the porch with large umbrellas. We were taken into the guest room. Looking at the magnificent wooden furniture and the maroon carpet, we were surprised. I wanted to shoot a few pictures there. The rosewood stairs and the portraits of royalty with swords hanging by their waist and candles burning motionless below them was grandeur in itself.

After sometime, we were called up for the dinner. I was afraid of meeting too many people upstairs. I was afraid of having to answer too many questions from too many people, especially when the questions would get personal. But, there were just the two of them waiting for us. It was a big relief. The old gentleman and his wife welcomed us. We were offered chairs and after sometime, our conversation kicked in. We exchanged our experiences with photography. I saw some of the best shots from India before independence, pictures of the celebration of the birth of the princess, hunting games, festivals, durbar decorations and much more. I exchanged some of photography experiences and time taken to shoot them in the wilderness. I was still clueless about why was I called for dinner until some day later I came to know that they were a big fan of photography.

After dinner, we were sent back home by the car. It was exciting. It was like being on board a ferry that took me to my dreamland and back. The next day, we narrated the details of our evening at the shop. Some were amazed, but some were indifferent – especially those that worked in the house and had already seen the life.

Cry Out Heart, Cry Out

We loved to spend time together in the woods, sitting hand in hand for hours. Most of the time, it was deserted. I enjoyed dinner with her, at her hut, with her mother. The silence, her presence, the night, the wood burning quietly in the fireplace, the fog, the yellow street lights, the rumble of the tin roof with the winds, and the looks she and I shared made it all so beautiful.

After dinner, we sometimes stood below the yellow street lights, or walked in the dark without uttering a word. We defined each other's existence in those moments. Sometimes, her mother would talk about her father at the dinner table. She seemed to be a very strong woman, and never let her daughter feel that she was missing her father's presence in her life. She raised her to be no lesser than a child raised by both parents, and she was proud of it. On some occasions, her mother spoke about her husband with pride, but so emotionally that she would begin to cry towards end of it. It would culminate in mother and daughter hugging each other, and me sitting there awkwardly. Whenever that happened, the night tended to seem heavier, and in our walks, the lingering silence grew heavier with each step we took. I would try to distract her, trying to take her mind off the things that weighed it down. I didn't want to increase her pain, so I didn't linger on the topics that were discussed at dinner. The melancholic winds whispered into our ears. I never wanted to show her sympathy to address her pain, for sympathy makes one weaker. Rather, I wanted to take her away from the pain altogether. I got her to take me to different places, so that she would be engrossed in explaining the history of the place, or some interesting fact about it. When I felt that she would best benefit from the silence rather than distraction, I left her alone. She needed silence, too, to put out the tempest in her mind. I didn't disturb her when we walked in silence, and for her part, she never spoke. It was hard for me to understand her silence. We would walk quietly, sometimes hand-in-hand, sometimes not. Sometimes, she would stop and hug me, and we would remain silent. Sometimes, she would raise herself onto her toes and hang onto me silently, by my neck. I looked into the dark, sending every thought in my mind away. I always wanted to look at her face when she hugged me. I wanted to know if she closed her eyes. Sometimes, she would sob silently with her head on my shoulder. I did know what to do when she did that. I wanted her to feel free with me, and to know that she could be herself with me. In those moments, I did think she did take liberties with me enough to let her-self go.

We would walk back to her place in silence. She would hug me again, and then swab my shoulder for her fallen tears. She would turn and go into her house, and I would wait outside until I knew she had gone in. I would leave in the hope that there would be better days, that there would be a time when she wouldn't have to cry, when she would find someone who would be there for her all the time.

"Sorry!" this is what she often spoke dimly. Then, she swabbed my shoulder for her fallen tears and she would straightway go inside her hut.

I stood alone under that yellow street lights either lost or in wait for her. But she never turned up again. My standing under the lights was a mixture of hopes that someday everything would be fine; that someday she might stop sobbing; that someday she might find a permanent shoulder not to sob upon; that someday I might find a way to make her stop crying; that someday she might come out seeing me standing under the yellow street lights alone in her wait and hug me one more time. She never came out after she went in, so I would walk back hotel quietly. Once in my room, I would listen to Gary Moore's "Still got the Blues". I wanted to find a way to help her out, but the loss of her father was an irreplaceable loss. There was only one solution: "*cry out heart, cry out!*"

With a mug of coffee, I would sit beside the window and look at the silent and dark landscape in the night with the cry of the guitar sounding in my ears. I walked through the lonely streets and dark valleys. The next day, snowfall followed. The sky cried with her.

Malana Meditation

Time seemed to be running slower for me. I was still a part of the same world. It felt like time had expanded, and that skewed perception it gave me allowed me to explore my existence in different dimensions. I was experiencing the world as a third person. I looked at my past with each passing moment. Time was no longer a continuous vector. It was a discrete one, now, where the minutest scale of time had finite values that could be seen passing by. Seconds and minutes existed, but they merged together into a new scale, which could not only be seen and measured, but also realized in real life. This was the effect of "*Malana*" Ganja over me. Time picked up momentum gradually as the after-effect of a puff abated. The moment, I took another puff I went back to seeing the same effect of time getting dilated.

For those who do not know, Malana is a secluded village situated at almost ten thousand feet above the sea level, in Kulu Valley in Himachal Pradesh. The name, Malana, is attributed to the river flowing beside the village. It is famous for its purple colored Ganja which grows at the higher altitude.

When I got home earlier from work, the tea-hut was where I would be. I saw porters returning to the valley after their work, at the tea-hut. They stopped to have their final meeting for the day over tea and make final adjustments to their loads before striding up the trail behind the hut into the valley.

I was fascinated by the culture of the valley. I walked behind the hut to see the length of the trail that would disappear somewhere amidst the long grasses and thick pines. The valley was not always enveloped with thick vegetation. On a clear day, I could see stretches of miles into the valley. The open fields and tiny figures lingering in the fields were a sight to behold. The more time I spent indulging my fascination, the more curious I got. Many a times, I was invited to the valley by the porters. But the demands of work and my monstrous laziness never let me take their offers.

One day, I decided to give in and went ahead. I was sitting on an old rugged carpet inside an old pine hut under a burning kerosene lantern and meditating over Malana with other porters.

I was given the chillum. I took it in my hand and closed my eyes for the first puff. I was cut off from reality almost immediately. I ventured into an imaginary place where time adjusted itself to a new scale. I felt my past moving and my present standing and withering away into the past at the same time.

I developed some cognitive senses which picked up on the few vibes out of the thousands of vibes floating in the air, that I synchronized with for the peace of mind. My ephemerally acquired sense picked nothing up but the silence. My eyes were closed but I could still see a sickle-like mark floating on the red flimsy canvas of the inner side of my eyelids. I was amazed. How was I still able to see something when my eyes were closed? I raised my eye balls to the top of my eyes and could not see a thing. It was completely dark over and scary. I puffed again and felt like I was dreaming lucidly, or perhaps, was in the midst of a lucid meditation. I found every reason behind all the bafflements that remained in my mind. I found the perfect way to get to her and to rescue her from this mundane world where emotions and humanity was a rarity.

I came to realize that masculinity drew love mostly from the attractions while feminism favored towards commitment. My wild experience steered into her intrinsic beauty. Her humane heart, her compelling eyes, the curiosity and innocence on her face, I could relate to everything connected to her inner beauty. I was connected to so many attributes but I was still able to figure out the thousand specialties that constituted her beautiful heart. I could feel the difference between my extrinsic and intrinsic worlds. While my extrinsic world was being shared with others, my intrinsic world was contained within me and that was when I got to find myself and, to lose myself within me.

Just to check my nerves and memories, I started retracing the path that I followed to the valley. Everything appeared blurred in the beginning. It was hard to focus on one thing. Everything looked so muddled. It felt like I had gotten a lion's eyes, since everything appeared black and white in front of my eyes. There was a herd of zebras and in the crowd of black and white stripes, I could not hold on to any one as prey until I saw one getting separated from the group. It felt like there was a cloud of dust being rattled up from the hooves and nothing was clear. It took time to settle down before I could retrace the same trail where I started my journey, and further back to the moment when I was being helped by the porters to pack my luggage.

Someone softly bumped my right arm. I opened my eyes. I felt like I was lost and had been sleeping for hours, though I was half awake. I looked at one of the porters beside me and he passed me the chillum again. The pine hut was filled with thick white smoke floating over the cold air under the yellow contrast of the burning lantern. The lantern glass was smudged in black by its burning wick. I puffed the chillum again. I felt the blood rushing into my heart. I felt the palpitations, ready to break my rib cage.

I exhaled the smoke and the surroundings became fuzzier. I felt my lips turning dry and scaly. I swabbed my tongue over my dry lips but it was of little help.

"Water...." I said as I pointed to the mug of water kept on the stool in the corner.

That was my only need then - to satiate my parched throat. I felt the coldness of the water as it rushed down my esophagus like gallons of cold water rushing inside a pump. I closed my eyes again. I saw heavy boots leaving behind deep foot prints on the soggy ground. There was no sun to take away all that beauty from the sleepy grass. The more we descended, the more beautiful the valley was turning into.

We walked and walked. The invigorating beauty and freshness of the valley was mellifluous, and sounded better than my favorite song I heard every night before going to bed. It was a heavenly abode. Angels do not fly here, and the rain sweeps pain when it falls hard on innocent cheeks. Ahead of us, there was a serpentine trail of crisscrossing pines. Pebbles crunched under our heavy shoes and the soaked, fallen leaves added to the wild ambience. The flummoxing beauty around, sliding mist over the hills, long trees peeking out of the mist in anticipation of better weather, and the grass that held pearly dew drops were all Mother Nature's very own creations.

Dark woods, the moth-eaten smell of soaked fallen leaves, some ghostly trees, and the mist brushing through our hair, It all added dimensions to the dimensionless awesomeness. A dark curtain covered the valley after the sunset. In the monsoon, there were torrential downpours at regular intervals and storms. Besides these times, gentle clouds hovered over hills and slid along ridges and valleys. One season would see trees laden with wild guavas and berries. Little kids would climb the trees and fill the valley with their shrill whistles and shrieks of happiness. You could never miss the wonders that surrounded you then, because every tree, every rock, every anthill, every ray of the sun and every star was filled with the wonders of nature. Life in the valley was filled with grace and a silent social harmony.

The vegetation, lifestyle, language and the weather, almost all of the biotic and abiotic factors tended to vary with the altitude in the mountains. With time, Shimla struggled to preserve its traditional values against a realm of modernity. Just miles away, the valley remained untouched by modernity. Locals who lived in the valley propelled traditional values of the mountains in Shimla.

Winter seemed to have marred everything on its way. There were certain winter flowers, pines, bamboos and grass, which were all fresh and beautiful. Branches and twigs slipped in and out of our way. We walked along huge pine trees. I loved it when our boots left their marks behind on to the wet soil. I loved it when grass lay crushed for a while under the boots and rose again. I loved the dew sitting quietly over white winter flowers, undisturbed.

I tried opening my eyes when I realized that I was too late. I realized that I was still roaming in a virtual world while in reality, I was sitting on earth. To check again, I closed and opened my eyes again. I saw people sitting opposite me and saw the world within them. I felt their hearts. With each puff, I felt as though my impure thoughts were sublimating along with the thick smoke.

People sitting around me were talking to each other. Some, like me, were quiet and lost. I snuck in silence despite the hum of conversation, and looked around. As I turned my neck to the left, I felt that the new scale of time had taken a new shape. With every turn I felt the minute gradients of an angle.

I looked in front, registering all that I was seeing. When I turned, the vision remained with me, and a new moment was being painted on a glass slab beside me. I turned little more to the left again. I always looked at the present, but felt that I could see the past from the corner of my eyes, preserved on a time slab. I felt like I could compare the configurations of the space against the time. It was hard to have a grasp over what I was experiencing. I could feel that I had miraculous cognitive power which was filtering my thought processes, scrutinizing the complex thoughts and giving me a reason for everything. Maybe because of that, I heard the silence in all the noises.

But, the world concealed behind closed eyes was so inviting that I decided to close my eyes again. I rested my head against the wall and went back to the valley.

So again! On the way to the village, we walked along a river. The day was neither sunny nor cloudy, but cold. Some of the porters would tell me how they almost met or narrowly avoided a leopard or a bear. I would not have believed them had I not read Ruskin Bond's works, or had not seen the leopard with my own eyes on my visit to Chail in Himachal, on a rainy day few years ago.

We had left the thick pine forest behind and were now walking along the river. I was told that the river descended from the Himalayas, perhaps because of its pristine and cold water, but I showed them the evidence that grounded their beliefs. I showed them rocks which were carried away by the river from the glaciers in the lower Himalayas. Sometimes, these rocks contained traces of Kyanite, a gem which looks like a blue-bladed crystal fitted into black granite rocks of the river. Kyanite is a result of high pressure and temperature produced due to tectonic movement of the Indian subcontinent which eventually, over millions of years, formed the Himalayas and pushed up Mount Everest as the highest peak of the world. It was not very hard to make them understand the geology of their space.

We walked further, and soon, the landscape changed as terrace farms came up. It was foggy in the valley. I turned around for another time and Shimla was almost not visible to my bare eyes, thanks to the fog. The valley was as silent as the still air, except for the sounds of the flowing river that warbled at random. Cold air sometimes froze one's ears. There were fields of carrots and cauliflowers to my right and to my left, was the river. The locals had constructed the road out of pebbles from the river. The pebbles were used to make a small barrier of water like a beaver dam. In the rainy season, the river crossed over all the boundaries.

Seeing my camera, a few kids ran towards us, dressed in jackets and boots. Their plain faces gleamed with ethereal joy. Sparkling eyes, soft skin, big coats hanging over their small shoulders: all put together, they were a source of positive energy for me. The kids smiled. With their fallen teeth, they looked beautiful and innocent.

I felt like I had a twin who was walking along with me in the darkness of the valley. It was just another part of my existence. He was a part of my bipolar nature, and craved always for love. He wanted a free life. He was an adventurer, bold and brave, and feared no death. He was free from all the complications of the world. He must have been a by-product of my failure in love. But he was like a younger brother to me. He treated me as a responsible person but he was too smart to handle the intrigue of the world. I never forced him to leave the mundane world.

The sanest people who bypass the social obligations are either called as intellectuals or the insane. I never wanted him to be misled by social nomenclature. He would mostly be doing stuff that was termed "crazy" by people who are regarded responsible and have experience. But there was no proof that the verdicts of the experienced and responsible people would always ring true. Most verdicts are influenced by stagnant and unmotivated consciences and if someone was talking about the craziness of my free roaming soul in the Twentieth Century, then chances were very high that he was devoid of motivation, thereby calling my free roaming soul insane.

I felt apart from my soul. I wanted to run away from my love, my parents, and my job, to find solace in nature. I wanted to spend my life on the mountains but that's impractical. While I would spend weeks sitting and spending life in a city, my soul would just want to fly high in the sky. Maybe that was why I always felt an urge to leave my job and run away in pursuit of my passion. Maybe that was the reason behind my aggressiveness when I could not see nature for a long time. I was on a quest for the truth behind everything. Why was I called insane? Why was I termed crazy? Why I was afraid of love? Why were people confused and bipolar sometimes?

I dug deeper into myself to find more answers. I needed more Ganja to catalyze the process.

With a tighter and longer puff, I saw the fumes rising out of the chillum. I felt my left brain tickling my nerves. I closed my eyes. I felt like I was connected to the universe, and felt a fissure in my skull out of which an energy beam was shot out of my mind. The energy connected me to the universe. I was able to hear the noise floating in the air. I was able to pick up the tune of the silence. When I grew silent again, I realized that I was silent for longer. Those who talked never stopped talking.

I asked myself a thousand complex questions and had the answers ready to them with all the evidences and explanations which I needed. It was a multi-dimensional experience, where I was free of being the first person and could see myself as a third person. I felt the past and its varying configurations, converting them into the present at the same time.

All the mysteries unfolded before my eyes: spiritual, personal and eternal. I saw the world arranged. The perfect relationship laid among the pieces I had put together. I found the answer to why I was afraid of love. I was trying to carry two versions of my life at the same time. I was trying to maintain a balance in between a free soul and a responsible soul. Maintaining a balance made me connect with the intrinsic and the extrinsic world at the same time. The intrinsic world was a child at heart and innocent at soul. The extrinsic world was responsible and sometimes, pretentious, sensational, and dynamic. In loneliness, when the free soul met with the responsible soul, there was a clash. There was a war within. There was nothing to mitigate the effect. The responsible one always gave up in front of the free soul because he was responsible. These responsibilities reminded me of the real lives of the people. Everyone has a free soul and a dream living inside their hearts but not all are luckier ones to find the correct balance. Some simply curb their dream to be responsible. I had a rebellion within, who was hungry for adventure. It asked for love and adventure but never money. That's why I met many girls but could not get with them because they were not as insane as I was, or they were not ready to fly into another world.

With the word 'fly', my mind switched over to the valley where my soul was still roaming. He was drenched in fog. He was laughing. He was happy, and was on the verge of breaking down. All the intense happiness carries pain, be it the birth of a child, deep in some emotional movie, lost in a romantic book or on top of a mountain. Tears rolled out, and always did.

I felt tranquil. I felt cold, as though intensity with which I was living life was seeping out of me like steam carrying out the latent heat and energy, rises above water. I no longer had a feverish mind. I felt as though I had found my purpose. I wanted to lie down calmly, call it to the effect of Malana Ganja or whatever you want, but it was like a meditation when I was dropping behind every unwanted element one by one and was feeling as light as a feather. I reached a point from where I never wanted to return. I also knew that the state I was into, was just a mere illusion. The hallucination would show you something and you, like a brave soldier, would be asked to return to reality, which was connected to the materialistic world.

I felt as though I always boasted of not being a part of the materialistic world. And yet, I found myself connected to the mundane world. Though I enjoyed nature and pursued my passion all the time, I felt that I was missing something. Though I regularly experienced solitude, I was still dependent on the materialistic world for most of my life. Even if I had detached from everything, the last few strings were harder to let go of. I had a responsibility, one that I assigned to myself. It was mostly social in nature, but was not connected to the essence of my life. It tended towards selflessness and devotion. Thousands of ways can lead to spirituality, and they might be different, but the essence remained the same: to feel spirituality within.

Where did spirituality come from? It was the hardship, discipline, devotion or abstinence from the materialistic world. But I realized it was a mixture of all of it. Maybe that's why different people chose different paths to spirituality, but the essence was common for all: to realize and to know the true purpose of life.

Some said that the true purpose of life was in devotion and selflessness, which came from self-realization and practicing abstinence. But the life a human being, irrespective of his nature of job, geography, religious and cultural practices, is always surrounded by some obligation to society and family. One way is to leave everything behind and devote the life for its true existence.

I reached the same conclusion. Most times, though I enjoy nature and my solitude, I still felt connected to my social and moral obligations. They work like hypnotism on me, and ask me to come back to the mundane world. I fulfilled the purpose of my life, but it had tentacles rooted to the mundane world where I landed up time and again. I wanted to break free. I wanted to fly higher. I wanted to see the null space above the sky. I was a free flying soul for others, but for myself, I was shackled to the worldly desires. Did that mean that time was just an illusion and we were all hypnotized by it? The more time one gets for his inner himself, he is likely to be the winner in the game of self-realization. From where does devotion come into the picture? Devotion is to surrender oneself to someone. But who does he surrender to? Maybe that's why religion and God came into the picture. People can feel spiritual power in front of which they can submit their devotion. The ones who leave behind the materialistic world were, in reality, going to devote them to the God. In the process of devotion, they would rediscover more and would earn more time to look within, while others find God in every human being, and devote themselves to humanity and its reformation.

I came to the same conclusion, that I was being hypnotized by time. I felt that there was a vicious circle in life, in which, after some time, people had lesser connections to the materialistic world while a few could break free and others remained a part of it. Those who were abstinent earned more time for their inner-selves and attained self-realization and divinity. Those who were selfless devoted their time in others.

I came out of my delirium. I was stateless. I looked around. It was dark. I heard the sound of the wind gushing through the small hole in the bamboo thatch of the pine hut. There were not many of us now. I spoke to them, but could not remember what I said because I was oblivious to it all.

The last puff was passed to me. I did not want to sip in the smoky air, but I did. Each word that came out of my mouth slurred. Everything was slowing down, coming to a dead-end, almost, beyond which no world existed. Or perhaps, I had not experienced those yet. I closed my eyes. Whatever I then said to the others seemed as though I had not thought of it before, and that the words just slipped out of my mouth. By the time I took control of what I said, they were followed by another series of words. I was completely out of control. I felt so dissembled that I just wanted to lie down. I was hardly able to pull myself up to the cot, and I needed help. I managed somehow, and saw them pushing a clay oven under my cot to keep me warm for the night. It was almost dead but still had some heat, enough for the night. I pulled up the blanket. It was heavy and I messed it up. I drank another glass of water. My lips were still dry. I felt as if I had just met my guiding light and needed rest after all the encumbrances of the esoteric consciousness I had acquired. I needed to settle down for the next day with new solutions in mind but could never carry forward those arcane wisdoms in to the new sunlight. The night disappeared into the dark and long hallucinations.

I saw the last two porters saying something to me. One of them was barely able to stand on his feet, leaning over the shoulder of another. I could see his smile and his hands holding my hand as though he was shaking hands with me. I had no energy left to gather myself together. I felt my hands dropping over my chest after the hand-shake. He dimmed down the lantern hanging near the door. The hut was almost dark. I pulled up the blanket closer to my face. He turned and glanced at me. He waved his hands and moved forward.

"Sirrrrr…," he said, turning back at the door.

I could hardly lift my head off the pillow.

"Good night, sirrrrrr……"

He shut the door. There was a shallow halo near the hinges of the door that slowly shrank when he closed it. There was complete darkness. I closed my eyes. There was a deep silence. I stayed put, lying on the cot and covering myself under the blanket, so I did not mess myself up. I tried to make sure I was in a proper shape. I tried to stare at the ceiling of the hut, but could not see anything. I felt my eyes half-open and ready to close to take me off to some wonderland. I had palpitations. The blood rushing in the veins in my palm left me feeling warm. The pricking cot under my neck, the cold air washing my left toe, the mild heat of the clay oven under the cot that touched my spine and the blanket rubbing on the ground: I felt it all.

I tried not to think too much. I kept my eyes closed. The world was spinning in a thousand directions. I was spinning too. I tried not to open my eyes. There was eternal peace in the cold darkness. I let myself break free. I was free. I was flying and flying and, flying until eternity in my dreams.

The Wooden Cottage

Each day in Shimla passed by like a blur. There was an unknown fear gripping me. My assignment in Shimla was fast coming to an end, and I was approaching the termination. I would soon be shifted to cover other locations. I had already couriered some of my work – and the response was simply overwhelming. The Sunday market at the lower Bazaar, the woods, the tea shops, the mountains, the people standing and milling about – I had captured everything there was to offer. I had to rush to Kufri to get a couple of shots in between – the rush was thanks to the weather conditions that would soon make the region inaccessible.

I was going to shift to Kufri the next day. I realized that I did not have too many days left. Everything seemed to be coming to an end. There was a constant sense of fear of losing her, and it began to take hold in my mind. The cottage was in the outskirts of the city, set at the edge of the reserve forests. The next morning, I was set to shift to my new workplace- the wooden cottage at the edge of the town.

"Are you shifting there tomorrow?" she had asked me many times over on the eve of my move.

"Yeah! The contract with the hotel is over and I have to cover more reserved forests. I will be there now for the next seven days," I replied.

"Who will then cook for you there?" I knew she always cared for me.

"Raam Singh or someone else, I think!" I replied.

"Okay. Is it a safer place? If you don't like their cooking, you can come here anytime for dinner or lunch. It's your own place," I knew how much really she cared for me.

"Yeah, I will, but I don't think I will have time for lunch. But I might come for dinner," I wanted to keep her heart.

"When are you leaving from Shimla altogether?"

"My assignment gets over next Saturday. I leave on Sunday by car to Kalka and from there I have a train back home," I replied.

"But if you do not like the food there, you can come here anytime," she said again.

She was certainly upset. I found her caring ways endearing, but sometimes, it made me feel bad. I wondered at the futility of it all – that was all going to end anyway. It was evident that the two of us felt bad. We did not say much to each other except for a few mundane things. There was a sense of nostalgia taking over – I had built attachment with everything, even the non-living things- the hotel, the window, the woods, the mall road, the lower market, her tea-hut where I spent a lot of time. It was all so tightly woven with all my memories, that it got harder and harder to not to get reminded of them. I felt like I was being divested of all that my memories had earned and all the emotions that I had accumulated over the past few days. It was a strange feeling. I felt like I was being deported against my will.

"When exactly do you leave to the new location?" she asked.

"After breakfast, tomorrow," I said.

"Okay. I will come with you tomorrow. I want to see if they've made proper arrangements or not." I nodded.

The next day, everything was packed and ready. Raam Singh was ready too. He stood by with the vehicle after loading the luggage. I stood outside the hotel, smoking. Just as I was about to leave, the manager gave me a bottle of rum and a pack of eatables.

"*Sir ji*! You always liked onion bread. Here in the box is *Paneer Pasanda*- that white creamy Paneer dish that you liked most and always used to order. We really enjoyed your pictures and we will always welcome you here," he said, and slipped the package inside the car. The bottles of rum were packed inside a jute bag.

We exchanged a look as he gently slipped the bottle behind my seat. She knew that I did drink. I did not know how to say goodbye. I smiled and received a lot of smiles in return. Raam Singh hurtled across the road, driving as though he was on a race-track. Waving hands at the ones we left behind, we were leaving the city. A wooden cottage was waiting ahead.

As the car made its way up the concrete streets, we spent our time looking outside. The Gypsy whirled past tall conical pines and conifers. Snow hung off all the trees and their branches and leaves. It looked as though someone had purposefully decorated the path for us, as though the two of us were proceeding to move in together, into our new house.

Gypsy stopped outside a cottage. On one side of the cottage was the entrance, which stretched off into a road inside. The house overlooked a hill, and there were snow-capped mountains lining the view. There was a garage at the ground floor. Above the garage, there was a large room, where I was to be housed. It was one big room, bigger perhaps than a two-bedroom apartment of the city. There was a wooden stairway that led to the room from the grounds outside. We parked the Gypsy and climbed up to the room with the luggage. It was like paradise: the place was beautiful. I loved the way the windows opened out onto the valley. The French Windows were taller than me, and the velvet curtains gave the room a cozy feel. There was a kitchen on one side. The floor was covered with a maroon carpet. Near the window that opened out onto the town, was a bed. It was large, and covered with a maroon bedspread as well. The kitchen and the bedroom were divided by a large translucent curtain that hung from the ceiling. I loved the empty space it all encapsulated. The room also had an old table, with a lamp and a candle stand, and an old typewriter. It soon became my favorite place. There was a fireplace opposite the table, near the entrance to the room. The fire place was big and had a grill and a chimney ran along the wooden wall up through the ceiling. We heard a dog playing downstairs by the guard's room.

"I will check the kitchen first," she said, as she walked up to the kitchen.

I was busy stacking my clothes inside the wardrobe. I then moved onto put my other stuff on the table.

"They look new! It looks like it is in working condition. Maybe you are the first guest here!" she said, looking excited.

I drew back the curtains and the view was spectacular. I could not resist.

"Come here, let me show you something," I said, as I drew back the curtain. The view stunned her.

"Wow! Look at that hill! Wow….it's awesome!" she said, astonished.

The view was magnificent – the brown hills contrasting with the bluish white tint of the snow, the gentle rays of the sun, and the silence made it such a beautiful piece of paradise on earth. We could see a couple of houses down below – some had the old architectural style, with ancient and paneled doors. Some were simple. All the houses had walls and doors in different colors – and the net result was a magical display. I loved the entire place – it was like a piece of dreamy paradise. I stood at the portico and strolled along the periphery. In my line of sight was Shimla, nestled in the heartland of a small chain of hills. Those hills appeared dark-brown in color. There were no patches of greenery, and no other color, either. The whole forest looked deserted. And yet, they had a contrast within their own palette of shades. The lower parts of the forests wore a dark, chocolate-brown color. If narrowed your eyes, they turned hazy and blackish. The upper part of the forest was light brown. The forests on the way stood obstructing the rays of the sun from the evening sky. Had all the sunrays touched the ground, the snow would have worn a thousand colors ranging from yellow to red to brown to scarlet to carmine, and many more in between.

At noon, with the sun straight up in the sky, the snow was a bright-silver. Different parts of the town depicted different moods of the city. Some shone. Archetype-window panes reflected the rays of the sun. Some smiled, the shades and lights portraying thus. Some looked as though they were shying away under the shade. Some looked outright sleepy, peacefully placed behind the hills. Some looked like they were sitting idle. Some looked playful and the darkest parts looked dull. There was a common circuitous road that slipped through the woods and connected the entire town. I felt like I was sitting up on the twentieth Floor of a restaurant. I could see the farthest point on the horizon – and the vast expanse of the value. We lost sense of time as we were lost in thought while admiring the view. I walked further to the edge of the portico. From there, I saw a vast mass of snow, lying orphaned. It spread across miles and miles along the valley. It was not shining. It was a mixture of a mordant and heinous kind of snow that scared me from a distance. The next morning, though, they looked beautiful.

"Everything looks alright. But still, if you need something, you should come. Do not hesitate okay? I know that you are a little shy, at times," she said.

I wanted to tell her that I would miss her, but I held back. I asked Raam Singh to drop her home. In their absence, I explored the whole space.

In the afternoon, Raam Singh and I drove for miles, exploring topographical sketches and finding pitching points for the next night's photography of the dark constellations. It was the last part of the "Being Wanderlust" journey. Her presence was missing. It made things look a little gray to me. The journey was tiring, but did not go in vain. We returned with a perfect final pitching point in mind. I felt lonelier than ever before. I was missing her presence. The silence was even more silent than it ever was. It was harder for me to withstand the distance from her. The next evening, we had to cover the longest jeep trail and pitch our camp before the night set in, with evil winds in tow. However, the day's weather suggested that the weather for next night might be better.

"Raam Singh, this is going to be a long night for us," I said, expressing my helplessness of spending the night alone in the cottage.

Though I had spent my entire stay alone still that stay at the cottage felt lonelier.

"Saab ji, I am not allowed to stay with the guests, or otherwise, I would have stayed with you and slept at the floor," he said.

"Can I suggest something instead?" He asked.

"Yeah!"

"You can go back to the hotel for tonight," He suggested me.

"Nah, I can manage here."

She was with me in my mind. I wanted to take her with me to camp out at night. She had never been out like that before. I decided that I would call her the next day.

There was a clash of thoughts inside my mind. It was mostly about her reputation. She was surrounded by people who were considerably orthodox. Of course, they respected us, but that was more for my passion and the kind of job I was into. Taking her out for a whole night on a camping trip might have induced prejudice in the minds of the people in the village, linking the two of us. I decided to ask to Raam Singh about it. I always admired him for his social and cultural experiences. He was from Kashmir and lived in Shimla. He had seen life from different perspectives.

"Is it okay if I call her to camp with us tomorrow night?" I asked Raam Singh from the window.

"Saab ji, choice is yours. She is an educated and intelligent girl and she can decide for herself," he said.

I decided to ask him what was worrying me most. "I meant, would it be okay in the wake of this society and all that?"

"Saab ji, let society say whatever it wants. You do as you please."

Kiss at the Night Camp

The next day, we began preparing for the camping trip in the afternoon. The boot of the Gypsy was fully loaded with all our camping gears – tarps, a utility bag, sheets, thermo flasks, some spare firewood, an axe to cut more wood if we needed, our sleeping bags, some packets of food and other assorted necessities. She was like a child, excited about the camping trip and putting things together for it. She questioned me about everything, her curiosity knowing no bounds. When I had the tarp in hand, she had a series of questions about it. "In how much time can a tarp burn completely?" or "Is it possible to cover a hot bucket of water with the tarp to keep it warm?" or "What if the tent is blown away by the wind?" I was amused, more than anything else, and answered her as much as I could. Our journey started when everything was ready.

I was not mindful of her reputation then. There was, though, always a sense of circumspection that haunted my mind constantly, about her. She was blithe and carefree. She had an argument against all the banal idiosyncrasies of this mundane world- *"If they never cared for you, why should you care for them? It should not matter."* Her life so far had imbued a sense of self-confidence and self-respect in her. Like most others, she was not wary of strange thoughts going on inside thousands of minds. One could never live up to such ideals as those. Life rolled on with her personal interests remaining within social boundaries. She was content with that.

Sometimes, even if you do not intend for it to happen, you do tend to care overly for something. This is because your unconscious perspective assessments demand more of your responsibilities, time and again, recklessly. It incites you and somehow you find yourself obliged to humanity. It's never our fault because, somewhere, suppressed behind our thoughts and past experiences, we have an affinity for it. Somehow, our past shares the same attributes that we see in the other person and we want to take care of them. This is how it works. She seemed so happy and uncaring about anything, and was not weighed down by any worry.

In winter, the sun tended to set earlier than usual. Soon, it was going to be dark and the woods had begun turning darker. With time as we drove on, it got darker and darker.

"Are you afraid?" I looked at her and smiled.

"No. Why should I be? I am with you," she said holding my arms and smiling.

I knew she had put a lot of trust in me.

After a few minutes, she turned to me and smiled. "Actually, yeah, I am afraid – but only a little. This is my first time camping *na*!" she said. I enjoyed the guileless and innocent side to her personality.

We neared the camping spot, watching the snow die out and the trail growing tougher by the turn. It was sunny that day, and much warmer than usual. We drove on, seeing that there was lesser snow lying along the trail. However, the trail itself had turned nasty. The ride became stiffer. There were some open spaces running along the trail, which comprised a ridge, beyond which there was a sharp fall in the relief, into a valley. The valley had a series of ridges that was partly covered with snow. The peaks of all the mountains were snow-capped all year round. Dark woods stood behind us. The sky was dimly lit by the setting sun. The clear and solid winter line ran parallel to the horizon looking remarkably like a shining sword. At thousands of feet above sea level, it looked like the horizon was the one that ran parallel to the winter line in the sky. Just as we unloaded all our things, she looked at me excitedly.

"Do you want to try setting up a tent?" I asked her.

"Yeah! I want to see how it's done!" she said.

"Okay. So these are the bamboo sticks. You need to fit them into grids with one another, diagonally. Then, you need to pitch the pegs and tighten up the ropes," I explained to her, showing her how it was done.

She helped me set up the tent and cover things up with tarpaulin. It was now time to chop up some dry wood for the camp-fire. Raam Singh was busy working on making tea for us over ethanol lamps.

"The first lesson is, never cut the green or live branches. Either cut a whole tree that is dead, or, cut the upper branches that will be dry. Understand?"

"Roger that, sir!" She was good at in finding out the exact and perfect words to use to respond at the perfect time. This witty behavior of hers always picked my attention.

"Good. Now, for the next lesson! When you chop wood, move the machete away from your body, don't move it inwards. Okay?" I showed her how it was done.

"Can I try it?" she asked. I liked her attitude of being unafraid of trying new things.

"Yeah, you can! But be careful. This one is a little heavier," I said, handing over the machete to her.

She tried it out. She seemed good – perhaps she had wood-chopping in her blood because she was the girl from the woods.

When you meet someone and accidently realize that you share a talent and finesse of a common kind with them, you find an obvious reason to continue being with that person. This is how things work. We were comfortable with our like-mindedness. Knowing the similarity tends to expand and share the common comfort space, and this is how we start ignoring the negativity and the flow of a relationship turns towards complacence.

The winds had turned the evening colder. The sky was still dimly lit. We set up our camp fire for the entire night and tightened up the tents and the ropes lest they be blown away. The wind continued to whisper into our ears. A thick log stood in the middle. Its branches and twigs twisted around in all directions. We watched the log slowly burning and waited for the night to fall.

After night fell, the logs were set ablaze. The woody mound was burning ferociously in no time. I had planned to shoot my photos only at midnight. In the meantime, I got busy roasting corn soaked in butter over the fire. She sat opposite me, on a stone across the fire. Raam Singh was busy cutting and piling up the wet branches around the fire to let them dry. She was busy scribbling something in the ground with a stick. I looked at her. Sometimes, she looked at me looking at her and we smiled. Again, she would be busy scribbling something on the ground.

Her face shone against the fire. I kept looking at her. Sometimes, Raam Singh would catch me looking at her. I would immediately signal to him, as if to say, "You are not allowed to intervene, please!" He would keep himself busy with something or the other.

Raam Singh had a fair idea of the constellations and the configurations of the stars. I wanted to take many random shots and then coalesce them all into a single photograph. I wanted to use that to show the whole constellation and to zoom in and zoom out play around with different effects. The game continued even after dinner. Time flowed. She seemed like an ocean to me: deep, anonymous and mysterious. When she talked about love, she talked a lot. And, she always meant real love- a single one. For her, there was simply no other kind of love that existed. We were still sitting opposite to each other. I expected her to speak a lot because she had been talking all the way up. But the night had fallen silent and she had fallen silent too. She broke the branches into smaller ones and one by one, put them into the fire. That was unusual of her. I kept looking at her in hope that she might turn to me and look into my eyes, but her eyes were riveted to the fire. I tried to catch her attention by messing up her artwork on the ground with a longer stick. She was not bothered. I did not know what I had to do to grab her attention. I did not want to break the silence either because that had a different charm.

After a while, she broke her gaze and looked at me, her eyes blank. She then looked right back at the fire, immediately after. Everything I wanted to do had to be done without creating a ripple in the calm waters. To sync my vibes in her, I tried to make myself a part of what she was doing. I went and sat by her side. I helped her break branches. I helped her round up the firewood and adjust the burning logs. Sometimes, we would look at each other. There was an exchange of smiles, too, but it was never enough to pave the path to perfect harmony. I did not know the key to unlock her mysteries. The best thing I knew to do was to hold her and rub her back when she cried with her head on my shoulder on nights. I put my hand around her. I felt her jacket – it was cold. She had no emotion on her face. It was not the first time, though. We had attained a certain level of maturity with time. I was divested of any thought, too. In moments like that, I always wanted to be a smart and intelligent man who could read the unlocked mysteries in her silence. But, like I said, I was devoid of thought. I leaned in to see her face. She was always aware of everything, or so I thought. She looked at me. Our eyes met. She smiled a bit. It was the same, jaded smile. With a soft clutch, she held my hand with hers. I could feel her grip, even if it was light. I looked at our hands and then into her eyes. She didn't say a word. She looked silently at me and then looked at the fire. My mind had given up all further thoughts and we sat like we were made to sit there, without knowing what would happen next. We held our breaths, trying to look calm and composed.

For me, there were two things to look at: her glowing but silent face, and the fire. It was more or less the same with her, too.

"What will you do after you leave Shimla?" she broke the ice finally.

I always found questions like this very perplexing because I had no answer for them. It was harder to imagine a turnaround from her. I looked at her and said nothing.

"Have you ever fallen in love?" she asked me again.

"Yeah, many times."

"How many times?" she asked.

"I don't have a count! I sometimes cannot understand what true love is! So, I really do not know if those were love or mere infatuations," I said.

However, each time I fell in love, it was for the better. I found each new relationship better than the previous one. Each girl was better than the previous and maybe that kept inspiring me to keep moving and fall in love again and again. Or was that I was maturing up by learning from my past mistakes?

"Have you ever felt true love?" She asked again

"Yeah, I think I did experience this with one girl. The real basis of love is to let go. It is 'bliss is ignorance' and 'Ignorance is bliss'! Just let it happen and let it go. Finally, it turns out to be 'let him go' or 'let her go'. They also let me go, but I could not let go. It was always harder for me to move on, but I learned and learned with each instance when I had to move on," I was trying to explain my complex and confused love life to her.

This was how my love life had been, always. I was never successful in love. I was always angry. I understood that those girls needed security and care. But I had never been good at providing that. There was always a clash of thoughts. I knew how to be, but I could not be a good lover.

"Who was she?" she looked more interested.

"Is that so important now, when we are here together?" I asked.

"Do you still think about them? You miss them?" she did not care for my question. She just wanted to know.

"Yeah, I do, sometimes. I told you it was always hard to move on!" I said.

"It hurts a lot. Right?" she asked.

"Are you afraid of love then?" I asked her.

"Yeah, I am," she said.

"It must have hurt you a lot, too. Right?" I noticed that she was pressing her soft hands against mine, as if she was trying to alleviate my pain.

"Hmm..." I said.

Silence prevailed again. The rustle of the leaves and dry twigs crackling in the burning fire filled the soundless spaces between us while we sat together in front of the fire.

I felt her looking at my face, as though she was trying to read my past and pain. I felt my face heating up. I could not move all of a sudden. I didn't know what to say. I was clueless. My gaze hung like the embers of a dying fire. I heard the vehicle door close. Raam Singh was busy making his sleeping arrangements in the middle seat of the car.

"Would you leave someone behind for someone new and better?" she asked me.

I could feel her gaze on me. I was numb, and kept looking at the fire. I turned to face her. I saw her eyes – they were full of questions. Dark, crimson glares radiated off her innocent face. She looked like an innocent child. Her eyes seemed to be asking me a thousand questions each moment. I extended my hands around her and held her tight. She closed her eyes. And, I felt like thousands of the eyes were shutdown at a time. I kissed her forehead. As I moved away, she opened her eyes and looked at me. This time, her eyes were not asking me any questions. They had gotten their answers.

"I don't want to run anymore. I am tired of running around and away," I said.

"Come close, it is cold there," she could never see me lost or trapped as she held my hand tightly.

Maybe she understood the enigma that was puzzling me. I had fought this war too many times, but I still had no idea why. There was no meaning in getting hurt again and again. People moved on but I could not. One of my feet always remained in the past because I felt connected with it. She understood it. I was lost untangling the knots of love and life. There were "whys and why nots" that always haunted my mind. Maybe that was why I always wanted to be away from people. I realized that all memories are linked to one-another. Every attribute that affects our lives in some way or the other is so deeply interwoven that each action has thousands of reactions. Each word that enters our ear carries a lot of attributes. Seeing me still lost, she tried to pull me closer. I felt the grip of her hand on my right arm. I sat closer to her. Very close.

"Do not think too deeply," she said, resting her head on my shoulder.

"I do not miss everyone in my life - but there is someone I always miss. I see her in every girl I meet. She was so close to perfection that I cannot think of anyone as being better than her and it is hard to move on," I saw her from the corner of my eyes sitting beside me.

"They have all moved on. Now you should get out of the past and move towards the future. Experience the present, forget the past," she said.

"Yeah, I suppose you are right. I understand these things now," I said as I wrapped my right hand around her tighter.

"You are not cold?" I asked her.

"Um-umm," she nodded. The fire had almost died. The embers were warm enough to keep us warm.

I looked at her. She put her head on my shoulder. Her eyes were closed. They were the same eyes that made me feel obliged to them. She had engaging eyes, and were the very ones I looked into when she wanted to say my name, but did not speak it. It was more like she was agonized and had called out my name with her eyes. When I looked at her, she looked so calm and peaceful, as though she had concealed all the wretchedness of this world behind her eyes.

I ran my fingers over her face slowly and then along the contours of her face and her soft cheeks. She held my hand and pressed it to her cheek and snuggled between my palm and my shoulder. She looked cute. I embraced her tighter. She hugged me too. I drew invisible figures on her face with my fingers. She closed her eyes when my fingers crossed over her eyes, to open them again and look at me serenely through them.

I allowed my fingers to slip a little further. I touched her lips with my thumb, running it from left to right. Her lips felt like petals in my fingers. I looked at her face. She was still unruffled. I ran my thumb over her lips again and gently squashed them. Her eyelids drew down. A tiny vibration surged across her lips and her breath grew warmer. I pressed down gently again, and I felt her shudder as though there were ripples floating across her body.

I leaned in and kissed her. I pulled her closer and pressed her body against mine. She was as close as she could be, to me. Her grip around my body tightened. She had closed her eyes. I felt the heat of her breath and the weight of her hands around my neck.

I touched her lips again with my finger. She quivered. I could not feel anything else. There was complete darkness when I closed my eyes and I simply put my lips on her lips. The kiss was the Elixir of Life. It was dark, a syrupy, intoxicating kind of darkness. I felt her lower lip sliding softly between my lips, as if trying to find a warm place. All my senses had either stopped working or were watching my lips work. Her lips were the coziest place I had ever touched.

"*Umm... mmm... mm*," she moaned, holding me tight.

The same fruit tasted better each time. Her momentous moan was so enticing that I lifted her onto my lap. She sat on my thighs and held my head from behind. With my hand around her waist, I pulled her against me. She was light and soft. I allowed her to rest her head on my shoulders and then slowly, I put her lower lip in between my lips. We were drinking the sweetest potion off each other. I kissed her deeper, the rose petal-like lips glided in my lips. I loved the steamy skimming of our lips. I stopped for a while and drew back to look at her. She kept her eyes closed. I wanted to see more of her heavenly face, but she didn't let me, as she pulled me again and wrapped her legs around my waist.

She leaned on my chest. I took support from the ground as I leaned backward with my hands behind. She rode over me and it seemed like the kissing was never going to stop. It was seductive. I laid down over the slightly warm rocks and she was above me. She kissed me and looked at my face, as if she was asking how the chocolate tasted. When she looked up, her hair fell back, and she glowed in the glare of the fire. I tucked stray strands behind her ears. The next moment when I looked up at her, she leaned in and began to kiss me again. She kissed me from my forehead to my chest, as if marking sweet stamps over me. I felt like her savior, like I always felt when she finally stopped and rested over my chest. She wanted to contain her inside me. I wanted to lie down and drift away like the blue smoke, floating lazily away, in the air.

The vigor was slowly dwindling off. I looked at her. She was lost and doped by the intoxication of the moments we shared. I held her tight. She squeezed and cuddled me like a baby. She had her legs on mine and her face was on my chest, closer to my chin. I put my hand over her thighs and slowly lifted them and put them over my legs. She was soft from top to bottom. Touching her thighs was like touching a slick cheese roll, just on the verge of melting. Everywhere I touched her, she felt silky and warm to my touch.

I did not want to move a single inch. I did not want to lose territory. I kept lying down for a few minutes, looking up at the stars and sometimes looking at her face, lifting my head up just a little. I would sometimes rub her back. She would kiss me in return.

"You don't want to sleep?" I asked.

"No," she replied.

"But its cold out here!" to which she cared not to answer.

She was lying down, looking at my face every now and then. I played with her golden hair and her glowing face.

After sometime, the fire had almost died out. I looked at her. She was comfortably sleeping on my chest. I quietly lifted her. She hugged me like a child. I took her to the tent and set her down softly on the air mat. By that time, she already had opened her eyes and kept staring at me in the dark. I found a sleeping bag in the dark and unfolded it.

"Slip inside. You won't feel cold, the ground is too chilly," I said as I passed it to her.

"Aren't you sleepy?"

"Yeah, I am, but I want to take some pictures and then I will come. Sleep till then," I told her.

She slipped into the bag. It must have been very cold. She shivered and hugged me. I kissed her hands and came out of the tent, closing the door-shade behind me. I set up the lenses and tried shooting some pictures, but the little fire was de-saturating the color contrasts. I wanted to get a darker background with the glittering stars over the canvas, but the fire did not allow long exposure shots. I put out the fire completely to take long-exposures. The sky looked like a black canvas on which stars appeared like glittering silver crumbs. The star-studded sky comprising packed galaxies looked like argentine talc, peppered with grains that were spread across the canvas of the sky. It was definitely another world. There I was, standing in middle of a cold glittery sky, looking up at it from the dark, cold earth.

Everything looked black – the chain of hills, array of pines, relief of the rocks, the tent and even the white Gypsy. I felt like that was how tranquil the world would be after getting completely annihilated.

I left my tripod in the open. I decided to wait until the morning for the beautiful sunrise pictures.

I snuck into the tent with my camera, not wanting to wake her up – but she woke up anyhow. It was harder to find things in the dark. I somehow managed to grab my sleeping bag. It was as cold as ice. I almost also shivered as I slipped inside.

"Are they cold?" she asked, half-asleep.

"Yeah. You have not slept yet?" I asked.

"I did. It was a short but sweet nap!"

"Good," I said.

I found space inside the bag. She laid beside me. I snuggled up to her, and ran my fingers across her face, trying to see her expressions in the dark. She looked up at me, her eyes cavernous. I grew bolder, running my fingers down the length of her arms, and then her back.

Lying in dark with a girl was like an ostrich's theory to me: when an ostrich would feel that there was going to be a sandstorm, he would bury his face into the sand below as though there were no storms. I could hear my heartbeats in the silence. I sensed that both our hearts wanted to break away, but there was something impeding them. I was trying to contain myself. Each movement I made had become significant. In my mind, they went through thousands of test-cases, which substantiated the course of the action. Sometimes, the obsession with someone can so be over-powering that we may over-rule the outcomes drawn.

"Why are your eyes open in the dark?" I asked, feeling her eyes with my hands.

"I am not sleepy!" she said.

"Close your eyes. You will find some sleep," I said, slipping my hand under her head. It was tough to turn with our bodies clumped inside the sleeping bag. After opening half of the bag, I felt free.

"Can I hold you?" I asked.

"If you are asking for permission, then, no," she said, terse and implicit. I was prolix and explicit. I did not hold her.

After a while, she moved closer to me.

"Oh....oh!" she said, trying her best to pull me closer as I showed resistance. She took my hand to put it around her.

The sleeping bag was cold from the outside. I snuck my hand inside her bag and reached her back. She was warm. I wrapped her in my arms and pulled her closer.

She was in a T-shirt and I was dressed in thermal wear. I rubbed her back slowly. It felt warm and soft like a rabbit's fur. Her t-shirt curled up around the edges as she moved and accidentally, I touched her bare back. It felt soft and warm, too. I began exploring. Her waist was curvy. I felt the crater that her back and waist formed at the junction of their meeting. She shivered as I traced the length of her back along her spine. She gasped every now and then when her breath caught in her throat. She turned around and held me tight.

I enjoyed watching her every move. Each time I ran my fingers down her back, she stiffened. Sometimes, when I touched her back, she dug her nails deep into my arms, the half-moons of her nails left imprints.

"*Umm....*"

She grabbed my arms and did not let me move. She kissed my face and my chest, and sometimes, held me tight and kissed me until we were breathless.

Her T-shirt had rolled up fully. With my both hands, I grabbed her. And the tighter I held her, the longer she would kiss. She gasped, almost on the verge of choking.

I held her close. The very next moment, she was under me. Pushing her hair back from her neck, I kissed her softly and then kissed her on the lips. She took my hand and put it over her soft belly pressing it down with her hand over my hand.

I softly touched her lips with my lips. The second time, when I lowered myself down to taste the same fruit, she smelled my breath and moved in closer by lifting her head. It was as though, she had surrendered herself to the most angelic felicity in me.

The next time I went, she tried to catch her breath. I felt the vibration of her lips. As soon as I tasted her, she latched my lips within hers. It was like a pursuit of embracing love before it could appear before her. It had turned into a game. I let her breathe my breath. I loved it. I loved it more than I could have ever thought I would. It was steaming hot. I was, by then, half lying over her and deeply drowned in the game of lip-locking. It seemed like the kissing was not going to stop. On her forehead, on her eyes, on her lips, on her neck and when I was just about to kiss down below, she held my head and made me hear her heartbeat. I let myself free. She ran out of breath and pulled me into her embrace and locked her lips with mine. She was not ready to leave me, for sure.

"*I…ove… uuuuu…*" she made some sound.

"*Whoooooot?*" I tried to ask with my lip locked into her

"*I ovee uuuuuu…*"

I felt like the wind had been knocked out of my stomach. There were sparks that engulfed me. I set myself free. She held her face over my face in perfect alignment. The blizzard had crossed the threshold. It was time to slack off, though the waves were still flapping around in our hearts and minds.

I was still lying over her.

"I want to be with you forever," she said softly, hugging me tight.

"I want the same too," I said.

Next morning, I came out and tried to put on my shoes. The lower half of the right shoe was almost soaked in dew. I looked at the rain cover of our tent. It had been holding thousands of round transparent dew-drops that had caught the orange light and glinted in the morning. It looked like it had rained last night, but it was only the dew at work. It was still little dark outside. Only the East direction had begun to see the traces of light, while the rest of the directions were still engulfed in the darkness. There was a vast curtain of midnight blue drawn across the sky, slowly lifting off the eastern part. With time, the canvas slowly had streaks of orange and the tints were intensified with every passing moment.

I focused my camera and looked through it at the transient colors of the sky. It was displayed like a magic show. Behind the hills, it was orange. The front was still dark. There was a pool of white clouds hovering over the valley concealing everything underneath them. It felt like a sitting on board a flight that was about to take off. When you are in it and the earth is visible, it will be hard to take our mind off the thoughts of daily life. Once the flight is swimming into the pool of the clouds, all the mundane thoughts are hindered by the clouds. The azure sky shows you tranquil hope.

The sky was gradually turning red. I saw the sunbeams hopping out from behind the hills. It appeared as though someone had covered the sun with tarpaulin and it had holes out of which the burning sun was sending its beams out.

I turned around and felt like I was a part of the magic. Darkness was being usurped and the mighty sun had done a coup.

Many clouds were being blown away by the winds. Along with the changing colors of the rising sun, the pool of the clouds also changed its color, slowly going from yellow to orange to crimson to red and so on. The soft clouds that were being blown away glowed silver in the sunlight, flying a good distance before disappearing into the cold, thin air. The valley looked like it was covered with translucent white silk because of the fog.

The rising peaks out of the pool of the clouds began to look bigger and more faceted. There were a few clouds, but only a few peaks that rose above the pool were seen for a while. Soon, when the sun rose, nature shone light on the series of peaks and chains of smaller hills and peaks.

The morning was beautiful. The rising sun, the beautiful, sleepy town sitting in the palm of nature, the calming charm of the orange rays of the morning and the myriad dew drops all made me wish that I had had more arms and many cameras to operate at the same time. I was lost in thought. I did not even notice others milling around. But, later, I came to know from them that they loved the dedication and the passion with which I was lost when I was busy taking photographs.

Real magic never lasts long. It is the lucky ones that get to see it. I decided to wrap up. I was sneezing and had a running nose. Last night, since I had slept inside an ice cold sleeping bag with half of my body exposed to the cold air, I had caught a cold. Smoking did not help me. We put everything back inside. Slowly, the sun rose and the day got sunny – but not very warm, since the winds were still biting cold. We reached the cottage around ten ó clock. I decided to sleep after the breakfast. She decided to go home, to come back later in the evening, by which time, I had wound up with a headache and a fever, thanks to being unable to withstand the winds.

Care Behind the Concealed Love

"Are you alright?" I heard her voice.

It was her at the door. I opened the door. She hugged me, as though she hadn't seen me for years and was waiting to fall into my arms again. It must have been the magic of the previous night.

"Niam! You are burning. I think you have fever!" She was always concerned about me.

"Nah, I was just sitting by the fireplace," I said, not wanting to let her take care of me. I had, truthfully, spent some time by the fireplace.

After breakfast, I had also slept for a bit – and could not sleep anymore after a while. I spent time smoking, watching the landscape outside the window and burning firewood. I tried to take some shots with my camera but could not find the perfect angle. Or perhaps it was just the state of my mind that made me less creative.

"Wait, I will make you some tea. Come here, sit!" she said, and drew a chair to set down before the fireplace.

I was given a blanket and I was sitting there like a child waiting for the next order from his mother. I loved her care. I had forgotten what the word care meant. Putting a log or two into the fireplace, she pottered about to make tea.

"Did you go out after breakfast? You should not have gone out, if you did! God forbid, if something had happened to you? Do you know someone here? No you don't right?" she mumbled as she worked.

"This year, the weather is a demon. Don't hesitate to call on me if you need anything! You should not feel shy about calling someone, you know. Don't be bothered by what society thinks or says. People here respect you and I feel proud to be able to help you. That guy at the corner outside has sent milk for you! Don't go out anywhere tomorrow. Sit indoors and do something. Have oats with hot milk, and some turmeric! Why would you speak? You never speak much, you are so shy," that was out of anger or she was just complaining, I could not figure that out.

I had never heard this much from any girl before. I could see my mother in her. She finally came out of the kitchen with two cups of tea. Turning the table lamp on, she put on a blanket over the chair and told me to sit. She wrapped me around with another blanket. I enjoyed the tea. It felt peaceful and silent.

Sometimes, when I was alone and needed peace, I switched off the lights and lay down silently in the darkness. Even the softest hum disturbed my introspection. I loved to talk to myself silently in the dark. I made no sound and all the talking would be going on inside my mind. I would be playing both characters: the speaker and the listener. There would be a flight of fancies and I would travel with them. I would black out unwanted moments in the past and cherish the happiest moments. I would do a lot of memory-bridging. One memory would spark off thousands of other memories. It was like selecting one memory out of thousands of possibilities. The selection would be based upon the suitability of the memory. The suitability would define a series of criteria and the most suitable memory would be chosen and flashed before my mind. That memory wouldn't last for a moment before the next one would be chosen. That's how a series of complex bridges were drawn inside my mind when I took a flight of fantasies. I would get the same feelings with someone I was very close to. I loved to sit and look into her eyes. I wanted no one to disturb me or rob away my peace of mind. There would be no tracking of time. I would sometimes think and staring at the ceiling and there would be no track of time. The next moment, I would get up to drink water and would curiously look at the time, and be surprised. Time showed that it had travelled a longer distance than I thought of, while I still lay in the same place.

I got up after sometime and switched off the lights and lit a candle. I loved listening to her. She continued talking, babbling about something or the other.

Though she spoke, the selection process was busy running in my mind. Each word passed into my mind through my ear, and a new memory related to the word came up. I loved listening to her, allowing each word to be accompanied with a picture. It reminded me of picture perceptions and word associations. She kept talking, babbling about something or the other. Listening to her felt like listening to peaceful music in the dark. The candles stood, motionless. On one side of the table, she and I were sitting together. Was it an illusion? I wondered. She sat there like a statue of divine kindness. I had not imagined that a kiss could ignite such love.

"You want to see something?" I asked.

"Yeah!" she said.

I got up and reached for my knapsack. I took out some old pictures of mine and turned the table light on again.

"So, this is how I looked, when I was in Class six. I studied at one of the most prestigious boarding schools in Mussoorie," I told her. We came to another photo.

"This one was taken when I was selected as the junior dorm captain."

We shuffled through the pile of photographs.

"This one was taken when I was in Class nine. You see this small kid? He and I were very close. Once, he was not on my team while playing cricket and he almost cried"

"Who is this small girl?" she asked, pointing to another photo.

"She is his sister. She was in class three then. Their father had gotten transferred and they were leaving school. I had gone out for an inter-school hockey match that day. They loved me so much, that they made their parents wait for me to return before they left. When I came back, he ran and hugged me. Since we had no pictures of each other, in a hurry, he gave me his sister's photo. He wrote me a note at the back of the picture, with his new address."

"Turn it over," I wanted to show her behind the picture.

"See? That small, not-so-bad, kid's hand-writing. He wrote his new address there and almost cried. I won't deny that there were tears in my eyes too when he was leaving and looking outside his car, waving his hands at me."

"*Bhaiya... Bye!*...... They shouted out, until their car was lost behind the woods and hills."

We spent many minutes talking together.

In the evening, she decided to cook me some dinner while I sat by the fire. She served me some delicious and hot food, looking at me while I ate. There was no definition for our relationship. But, we had travelled too far, by then. In India it was very tough to define this kind of a relationship. People meet, people kiss, and people are in love: but it seldom lasts long.

There was no looking back. There was a reason why we met. We were together not knowing how long this was going to last. We cared so much for ourselves, and there was an inherent apprehension that things may not turn out as we wanted them to. We just wanted to let go of each other because there seemed to be no reason in continuing together, though there may have been a reason that we had not thought of. There were two wills: one of being together and one on moving on when there would be no ideal solution for the first. We were afraid that we were already into a complicated situation. She was determined about her mother making a choice of a life partner for her. I was not willing to give up my dreams and career. We sacrificed our personal choices for the benefit of other things.

After dinner, I decided to sleep. She arranged her bed near the fire place. I insisted on her sleeping with me. She put off the candles and sat beside me.

"I can't see your face," I said.

She drew back the curtain. I saw her face under the light of the street lamp-post. I adjusted my pillow and lifted my head. The whole town was visible. It was a cold night. I felt like I had gained wings when she sat beside me. I was flying over Promised Land where people went after Nirvana. Shimla looked burnished from a distance. It was like a Roman stola that had spread over the dark hills. The stola was peppered with small lights and soft glows. I saw the reflection of the town in her dark eyes. Her eyes were shining and were exuberant. I felt her hand clutch my wrist. We were hand-in-hand again. She smiled. Her smile was evanescent, like sparkles illuminating the air around. She touched my forehead and ran her hand through my hair. Then, she slowly ran her palm over my eyes.

"Do you have headache too?" she asked, running her fingers through my hair. I did not reply.

"Does it feel good?" she asked, running her fingers on my forehead and pulling my hair softly, as if to alleviate me of headache.

"It's okay. Just be here. I feel good," I just needed her around me.

"Yeah, I am here, don't worry. Do you see that lonely yellow light alone to your left through the window?" she asked.

I turned to my right and asked her, "Which one, the one on the left most at the top?"

"Na! A little more to the right," she replied.

"But, I can't see anything to the right," I told her.

"Maybe because you are lying down. Let me take a look at what you can see," she came closer as if she was trying to measure what and how far I could see while lying down.

I looked at her face while she tried to trace the special yellow light that she was trying to show me. She held my wrist throughout. As she leaned in closer, I wanted to hold her again. Her hair fell over my face and the scent of her body was enticing.

"Now I can show you?" she held my hand in her soft hand and pointed to a lonely lamp far in the distance.

"That one!"

"Don't you want to rest?" But something else was on my mind. I wanted to hold her. It was hard for me forget her warm and soft body.

"I am here with you all night. Do not worry, I am with you," she said, as she leaned in and put her head on my chest. It was getting harder to contain my soul at one place. It was trying hard to break free and wander in a thousand dimensions.

I tried to look at her. I could not resist myself. Soon, I began running my fingers in her hair. I felt like I was forgetting many things at a time. My space was contracting and eventually, it would be just she and I left alone in the world. An unending rapture was being created. I never wanted to come out of it. I held her in my arms. She squeezed herself into my embrace and smiled. She closed her eyes.

"Niam.....!"

"Umm?" I replied

"Niam.....!"

"Umm?"

"I love taking your name. Do you know when people reply saying 'umm'?" she asked.

"No," I said.

"When they are in love," she said, and slowly looked up at me and smiled.

We had not explicitly expressed anything, but had accepted that we were in love. It was definitely love. The signs were clear.

"Come closer," I said.

"Can I touch your cheeks?" I asked.

"Mm-hmmm," she said.

"When do people say 'Mm-hmmm'?" I asked.

"I think when they are in love!" she replied.

"Mm-hmmm!"

"Would you leave me for a better girl?" she asked innocently.

"No. I am tired of running thousands of miles. I want to build my camp now. Can I kiss your hand?"

"Mm-hmmm." I kissed her hand lightly and that relaxed her. In the dark, she moved her hands over my face. Sometimes, she would rub my forehead.

"You are warm!" she said.

"Yeah," I replied. "Will you sleep with your head on my chest all night?"

"No. Not until you sleep!" She said, and closed her eyes. I closed my eyes and squeezed her tighter to me. It was all so peaceful – like sitting beside a silent lake on a warm winter day.

I ran my fingers through her hair, looking at her face. Sometimes she opened her eyes and looked at me, and closed her eyes again, lying down calmly. To keep the conversation alive, I asked her, "So, you were showing me some places of Shimla?"

Then, she sat and we looked out of the window again. It had gotten a little darker and had started snowing.

"Aren't feeling cold?" I asked her again. She looked up at me quietly, as though she wanted me to find the answer I was looking for in her eyes.

She didn't look away; it was as though we had known each other for years. Her calm and placid face appeared as though she had abandoned everything in life and had begun a journey of blessed goodness. She spoke, finally.

"I am feeling cold, but I don't want to go away from you."

"Then stay with me, but sitting this way is not good for you if you feel cold."

"I know, but it's okay," she replied.

"Please? I can shift a little and you can sleep here comfortably. Are you feeling shy?" I asked.

"Why do you always think so deeply? If I was shy, I wouldn't have stayed!" she said, as she hugged me tighter.

"Sometimes, you are caring but you try not to show it. You are a certain kind inside, but you try to appear different outside," she said.

"Listen! You should not be sitting here all night. You can lie beside me like in the valley," I said. I couldn't help but think that she was still a little shy about lying beside me.

She sat against the side wooden frame of the cot, putting half her body under the quilt. I laid down, putting my head on her lap. She ran her fingers through my hair. I looked up at her now and then, exchanging peaceful smiles.

"Do you still have a headache?" she asked.

"No."

"Sleep, then. Keeping yourself awake is not good," she said, touching my face gently.

"When I was a child, I had a few crushes but never found one I loved. After my father passed away, I began believing in miracles and had an imaginary guy in mind. It's not like there are no nice guys around, but I felt something special for someone I had not seen yet. Liking someone is one thing but loving someone is a special thing, right?" I liked it when she talked about love.

"Mm-hmmm," I said, listening to her raptly.

"Love cannot happen every day. It just happens. I don't know why people search for true love or match their compatibilities before loving. That sounds like a bargain and an act of selfishness. Even if you are the most comfortable with the most uncomfortable person, it is also a kind of love. People are not wrong! Maybe they are just looking out for the comfort in love," she said.

After some silence, she continued. "You know this world! People use you in the name of love. There is no value for anything – love does not last forever. Sometimes, arranged marriages are the best. It is like a bargain where you can still play the deal even if you have lost the game. Love marriages are where you think you win, but there is no guarantee." She was silent again.

"I am ready to lose everything for someone worth it. Girls must be throwing themselves at you. You are an adventurer, a nature lover, a photographer and so much more! I want to know about your past. Tell me!" she said, turning around with a defiant look in her eyes.

"I feel sleepy. You keep talking, I'll just nod off here for a bit." Though I really was sleepy, I did not want her to stop talking. She came close to me and kissed my forehead.

"Okay. I will keep talking. I had never imagined that someday, someone like you will be lying with your head on my lap."

"No, don't talk about all that. Just talk about love. I like your talk." I wanted to sleep, listening to her talk about love.

"Ha-ha, okay! You sometimes explain your life during your Masters. I liked your life. Sometimes, I find an inference with some mathematical formula that you use for making me understand life."

"I have always loved your thoughts on love. Love is a stochastic process for me. Your past doesn't change your future. It's only dependent on the present. Sometimes, the elements from the past are carried forward in the form of memories into the present. That's when things get unpredictable. Anyway," she trailed off.

Silence prevailed for a brief few moments, and she continued. "I don't like it when you ask me permission for everything you do. Can I sit? Can I sit next to you? Can I take your photos? Can we stop for tea? You are so confused about everything! Is it because of your past? I want my love to just do it! Do not ask me how!" she went on.

I tried to listen to her, but I drifted in and out of sleep, listening to her in patches.

The next morning, she was curled up in bed, looking like a kitten. Her hand rested on my chest. I found my left hand wedged under her cheek. She must have taken my hand and held it to her face while she slept. I did not want to wake her up, so I let my hand remain there. She looked like an angel who had gotten tired after doing a lot of work to save the earth. I wanted to kiss her lips, but instead, settled for gently kissing her forehead. She opened her eyes and looked at me peacefully and went back to sleep again. I liked that very much. Was it a gesture of acceptance? I could not wait to find out. I kissed her forehead a second time. She opened her eyes looked at me and closed her eyes again. The third time, I kissed her lips. When I drew back, she woke up.

"Are you fine now?" she asked, sounding sleepy.

"Yes, I am. You sleep, I will make us breakfast." I was living the life I dreamed of living. I could not think beyond a little cottage, a vehicle and her, all together in a beautiful, peaceful hilly place.

By the time I finished cooking, she had woken up fully. We ate our breakfast looking at the valley. Later, I dropped her home and left with Raam Singh to say thanks to the local authorities and to meet some others.

Shimla Revisited

Shimla had always been something of a fantasy to me. There was a layer of abstract beauty in everything, material and non-material in Shimla. I was so touched by the beauty that I saw in everything, living and nonliving. The narrow stairs that snaked its way through the lower bazaar, the tunnels that connected parts of the city, the wet streets and children playing in white snow wearing black coats looking like baby penguins, the snow melting over tin-sheds and dripping overnight - everything made me so happy. Raam Singh drove through the narrow streets. No one knew the labyrinth of Shimla better than he did, I suppose. It felt like it was the last time I was touring Shimla. I was never that much attached to any city I travelled to. When I went to Rajasthan, apart from the architecture and the culture that was preserved in the older part of the state, I was never interested in anything else. I had no reason to be so obsessed with anything – but with Shimla, I had a reason. The silky afternoon, the long shadows, the sloppy grass, the wooden houses, the colorful shawls displayed on the streets, so many people, and so much serenity- it was a whole lot different.

As we drove through the streets, every little thing I looked at made me feel like I was connected to it. They reminded me that I had a lot of photographs from Shimla – and despite that, it still felt inadequate. I realized how hard it was to do that adequately, given the riddling beauty that shrouded everything in the place. A photographer's work is always the preservation of something, and most often, each photograph is a preservation of inexplicable beauty. And evidently, no amount of photos would ever be enough. There was still a lot in the world that was left to be addressed. We had not even captured a fraction of the vast beauty.

We met some people and moved on to meet more. It was a thanksgiving visit.

I began exploring the world many years ago, and it was amazing how it was shrinking. But at the back of my mind, I knew that the descent was going to start sooner or later. I was going to miss my friends. I would be left with memories, and the dreams of visiting them again. This was what my life was meant to be. Like an adventurer on a journey, you cross one peak and walk over to the next ones. On the way, some things remain etched in your mind. Everybody sees the snow lying on top of a glass house, but only few see the slim rainbow lying above the glass ceilings.

One can never forget the wonders of nature. For me, it was impossible to forget certain things: the girl, Raam Singh, the window in my hotel room, the blue water flowing in the valley, to name a few. I realized that a month was not a short period. With each final bye and thanks to everyone who was a part of my journey, I felt as if though I had collected so many gems in short period of time but, I was losing them one after another.

One could not carry more than need. I just had to keep special ones and I was sure I was going to keep them safe forever in my heart and my soul.

The Last Night

Do you know what an explorer hates the most? Sitting idle and having nowhere to go. After thanksgiving and meeting everyone who was a part of my stay at Shimla, I was back to the cottage. I sat alone, preparing reports and selecting the best photographs for the presentation I would give soon ay my office. I had nothing to do much other than cooking, playing around with the kids, driving around town, meeting people and after sunset, looking at the town from the same window. In the grass lawns in front of the cottage, Siya and I used to sit together when it was sunny. We would not speak a single word for hours. Maybe our hearts did all the talking. I would sometimes feel a sharp surge inside my heart. What that surge was about, I did not know. Perhaps it was the fear of losing her. I never understood that. Sometimes, the dog would join us, wagging its tail and looking at us. We drank cup after cup of tea.

"So, what are you going to do after you leave?" A question from her for which I had no answer.

I wanted to explain why I did not have an answer left for her. I wanted to tell her that I could not think beyond the cottage, Shimla and her. I had no clue of what I was going to do because things were always changing. I was surely not going to do the same things I did earlier. Her question haunted me as much as it haunted her.

A letter from my friends would read: "*Dude, every arrangement has been made. We are coming to receive you on a Royal Enfield this time! Don't forget to bring that Malana stuff and some golden apples. Man, one month felt like years! Keep yourself alive and do not slip off again!*" But the entire meaning it held for me had changed.

Now, she stood on one side and the rest of the world stood on the other side. There was a clash of ideology. Raam Singh used to understand the frequency of our silences. Sometimes, he would play light music or sing local folk songs. It never helped us though. They were never deep enough to touch the abysmal depth of our hearts, nor were they enough to stop the flood of emotions within that were raging to break the barrier. They worsened my emotional urges. Though we understood each other's agony very well, together however, on our own sides, we were skeptical about our future. No degree of understanding was working out. We were from different worlds. A volcano and a tornado might possibly meet, but the result would be devastating. The tension of losing each other was always on the rise.

"I will make us some more tea," she would say, and then go inside, only to come out with red eyes.

I knew she sobbed silently when alone. I could not force her to stay with me nor leave me. She would leave in the evening and come the next morning, spending time with me until I would get busy in preparing submission report. I sat alone in the night beside three burning candles to prepare my reports. Lost in an abysmal silence, my mind was overwhelmed with the complexities of the world and I would find myself standing near the window looking at the city from a distance. Looking at those hazy yellow street lights brought me some relief because I had developed some unperceivable bond with those lights, too. I could describe my condition as that of a drowning person who just held on to anything that gave him hope in some way.

Saturday night was chosen as farewell night. She and I decided to cook dinner for some of our guests, which included a few guys from the hotel, Raam Singh, the guard and other native people we were familiar with. The party was unique. Everyone gathered in the evening. It was raining lightly outside, everyone talked and laughed, and it was a happy moment. We walked down the memory lane, and were rather emotional. The table beside the window was flooded with people looking at the photographs. The hotel helped us with the dinner. Siya had decorated the house with candles. Each sip of wine found a new wave of nostalgia floating. Each loaf of bread was a throwback to more emotional exchanges. The amount of open love that I received from everyone there was just overwhelming. There were no arrangements and everyone did what they wanted to do. Some sat on the floor, we didn't turn on the lights for a while. There was a lot of warmth among all the people. Old and rugged overcoats hung in the corner. Candles were burning around the room. Lazy wisps of smoke floated in the air. The smell of food cooking filled the room. I found it to be a mixture of savage but communal celebration.

Later, it started raining and people wanted to leave soon, lest they would be trapped by the rain. No one wanted to face the cold night. After dinner, as everyone began to leave, I started feeling nostalgic. I was leaving forever, the next day. I was the one who was going to miss the place the most. I would be the one who would look at the photographs and remember each moment spent there. That evening, I also tried Malana, and was pretty high by the time the party ended. It was getting tougher for me to keep my emotions in check, but I managed somehow. At the end of the party, the hotel staff helped me clean up the place. I sat down by the fire on a chair. Everything flashed before my eyes and began to run like a fast-forwarded movie with my favorite scenes. I wanted the scenes to be repeated. Some memories were such that I wanted them to be repeated over and over again. I don't remember why I was cheerful with everybody else. I think I was just drunk. There was some special French red wine brought by the staff of the hotel. Containing my emotions was getting tough for me.

Everyone had gone except for her. She came up to me. The room that was once filled with laughter and smiles was dead silent. One could even hear the cold wind whispering through the windows and the muffled sound of her foot-steps on the carpet. She stood to my left. I looked up at her. She put her right hand on my left shoulder.

"Are you alright?" she asked me.

"Yes!" I replied.

It felt like I had no connection with her anymore neither I was going to have any kind of connection with her henceforth. It was a guarantee that everything was coming to an end. It felt like it was just an infatuation, or perhaps confusion. One thing was for sure, though - I was going to miss her.

I had turned so ridiculous that I removed her hand from my shoulder and asked her to go home. I was tormented inside. Time seemed to have ripped apart the purpose of my existence. I just wanted to be alone. I was not prepared to face the future. Or maybe, I just wanted to slip into the future, leaving everything behind and embracing the unseen. Yeah, it was true that I had begun to see my future with her every now and then. She had make a good mother, a good wife, a good friend and a good lover. I saw myself happy with her in the future. Still, there was something pulling me back.

She, standing behind me, looked at me silently. I did not know how she felt. The way I was trying to suppress my anger was stressing me out. I did not want to ruin her last night and repeat those same mistakes that I had been making for years. I turned around and looked at her. She was silent.

I can't deny that she might have had some repressed thoughts in her mind. Life had taught her ways to compensate hurricanes in her path. She stood there, calmly.

"What are you going to do after you leave?" she asked me again.

"*I am going to die. Why don't you go away? Please!*" I almost shouted.

She was not the best at understanding another's thoughts. It was never her fault.

"Okay. Don't answer me. But don't get tensed, please!" her over-caring nature was now bothering me. I could not stop myself. In one go, I blabbered everything that was inside my heart for weeks.

"*I met you. We liked each other. We did not expect or promise each other anything. Now look! We met, we became friends, you accompanied me, you trusted me, and I trusted you too! This is how life is! You meet. You become friend and then you go away. There is no market for your emotions in this world. Maybe you might find someone better than me. I like you a lot and I even know that you like me. But do you see the point? We are from two different worlds! I am a free soul. I hate the uncertainties of life and love travelling and who loves being independent and dislike it when someone tries to clamp him down. You have lived your life in a world which has had love and positivity all around!"*

There was silence for a while.

She was not broken by my harsh words. She stood with the same placidness on her face.

Not to be denied, I was feeling relieved in a few next moments. I think I just needed to shout out my anger. Soon, the tempest was over and there was silence again like the silence after the hurricane. I was perplexed by my own absurdity. I felt cruel. I drank some more wine. She had a choice to go, but she chose to stay with cruel me.

"Please do not curse yourself. You are nice at heart. I don't know what makes you so confused and aggressive at times. I know you are caring, but sometimes you pretend like you don't care for me, but I know that you do. Your mind drives you. It's because you are afraid of hurting me. You are afraid of giving me any expectations so you want me to go away," she said.

"I never asked for anything. I liked your free soul. I never asked you to be dependent on me. Yeah, I know, we met and became friends. We even know that we like each other. You should not curse or blame yourself for such nice things. It is a part of life. Do not worry, Niam!" she said.

"But still, I mean, you are not going to be with me always! I see no point in being with you right now," I said, hesitatingly.

"Okay. If you want me to go, I am leaving, please take care of yourself. I never knew that we would have such an abrupt end." She put on her overcoat and I could see tears forming in her eyes.

"But please take care. You are drunk and please…." She could not utter more than that.

I knew she was pretending and I was pretending as well. We never had acted this formally before. She closed the door behind her as she left. I could hear her breaths, while standing on the other side of the door. It was still raining outside. Some silent moments passed…

"*Why don't you go to bed?*" she shouted from outside.

"*Why don't you go home?*" I shouted from inside.

"*I will go, don't worry for me,*" she replied.

"*Don't worry about me, either,*" I shouted, holding the door.

"*Then be alone! Goodnight*!" she said.

I heard her footsteps fading away slowly.

"*Yeah!*" "*Yeah! You also sleep alone tonight. Good night!*" I shouted from inside.

After a while, I rushed to the door just to take a look outside. I opened the door and looked outside. She stood on the ground under the lamp-post in the cold rain with her back towards me. That night, she must have cried. The sky did, too. Whenever it rained, she believed that the sky shared her happiness or sorrow. Sometimes, she turned her head around and looked at me while I stood at the door, looking at her.

"*Hey!*" I shouted. She stopped abruptly.

"*Can I have a hug for the last time?*" I shouted again.

"*You are forgetting something I told you on the night when you had fever. Remember what I said?*" she got me thinking.

"*No. I don't,*" I replied.

"*Okay. You don't need to ask my permission every time,*" her voice was shrill.

It felt like she would break down at any moment. She stood near the gate. She turned around. The lamps threw their light on her face. I saw light on her cheek and silent tears getting lost in the rain. I saw raindrops rolling down her cheeks slowly. I found a child in her: a child who never went against the will of her parents.

I could not wait. I almost ran up to her. I felt like a mother who had hurt her child – and watching that child standing far and crying for a long time, my heart melted and I ran to pick her up in my arms. She was like an innocent child, waiting for her mother to come and pick her up. I rushed up to her and hugged her. She embraced me like she had been waiting to see me for years. She was like barren land that had not seen a rain for a long time. I knew that she would come running to me, and that she would wait until I showed up. The moment I hugged her, the barriers that kept her emotions in check burst forth. She hugged me like there was no tomorrow. She could not contain herself and began crying like a baby on my shoulder.

"*Leave me alone! I want to go home,*" she shouted.

"*I told you to leave me!*" she tried to push me away. The harder she pushed, the tougher I became in order to calm her.

"It's raining. Come inside!" I knew it was not that convincing an argument.

"*Why are you worried about me? You are a free soul, why don't you just fly away? Don't bother about me. I am used to these things. I was always a trouble for everyone.*" she shouted, standing in the rain and getting wet all the same.

It took me a minute to carry her and hoist her onto my shoulders and bring her into the room. We were soaked in the rain and she was shivering. I lit the fire in the fireplace. We were still shivering.

"Mad girl!" I muttered under my breath.

"Who started it? I just asked you what you were going do after you left from here, that's all!" she said.

"I don't know. Maybe I will take a break and go to South India for a week or two. I will celebrate this success!" I said, and went to the corner of the kitchen for more wood.

"You should dry yourself and change your clothes. You are soaking wet," I told her. .

She went behind the curtains to change her clothes. Meanwhile, I got dry too.

"How are you feeling?" I asked.

"Warmer but I think I am coming down with a cold," she replied.

"It's cold outside! Some smart girl went and jumped in the Atlantic Ocean and waited for a man to rescue her, and in the process, almost froze to death," I joked, feeling playful.

"And who asked the guy to jump into the Atlantic Ocean to save Rose from the Titanic?" she joked.

"Okay, this was the choice the guy made because the girl is sometimes too adamant!" I retorted.

Outside, the rain was torrential. It made strange noises on the tin-roof overhead. I was scared at times, but she wasn't, for she was used to the rains.

"Last year at this time, it was the same. It was a scary night when it rained like this. Mom and I could not sleep the whole night. The next morning, we saw that there was a cloud burst in Upper Himachal and many people had lost their lives. There was a huge flood in the valley." she said, looking at the ceiling.

"Don't worry. Nothing will happen!" she assured me.

In hill stations, when there is heavy rain, usually there will be an accompanying power cut. Almost as if on cue, my thought manifested. The lights went out.

"Come here, I want to show you something," she said to me after we spent a good amount of time in the dark in silence. In the weak light of a torch in her hand, I noticed that she was wearing my bathrobe.

It was loose for her. She looked like a little child dressed in her father's clothes. She was almost drowning in the loose robes. There wasn't much light in the room. She drew back the curtains from the window.

"Now look!" She focused the torch light through the window, into the rain.

It was completely white.

"Can you see how heavy the rain is?" I saw some vague dots of light in the distance.

For the most part, the view was blurred. White streaks of rain fell from the sky. I was awed. The lower parts of Shimla still had some light. It did not appear as distinct units of light to our eyes, though. It seemed a little blurry. The rain was falling along the window panes. The blurred white and yellow lights slipped along with the water.

"If I want to show you something, would you like that?"

"Of course! You are allowed to do as you please until you hurt the feelings of a woman and do not harm her self-respect!" She was smarter. I respected her.

"Okay! You have to presume that we have known each other for years. I promise I will be within my limits. So, are you ready?" I asked.

"Yes, I am," she looked excited and a little nervous too.

"Close your eyes!" I ordered her. I stood behind her and covered her eyes with my right hand.

"Now walk with me." I said. I gently guided her towards the city-facing window and pulled back the curtain with my left hand. I felt her eyelids move under my palm, and a part of her soft cheeks as well.

"Now open your eyes," I said, drawing back my hand.

"Do you find it beautiful?" I asked.

Maybe, I was forcing an aesthetic sense on her, something she may not have been ready for.

"Yeah, I can see but…" she trailed off. I wanted to show her what I could see.

"Okay. I will tell you something and you have to imagine seeing it. Put on a shawl, you are still shivering," She did as I told her. I continued, "Imagine that this window-pane is a door to another world. Imagine that the rain stops and we open the window. It opens into another world which is totally different the one we are in now. It looks like the mysterious gates of the movie, Matrix. Instead of Shimla, it is a light, purple-colored world with lots of blue and violet color flowers. The tree trunks are also purple. There is someone waiting for you with a violin. Just outside the window, there is a maroon carpet leading to the shadow of a round tree in perfect shape. Can you feel it?"

"Yeah! It looks romantic," she closed her eyes.

"Forget the drops of rain; forget the sounds that are coming from the surroundings. As you step out of the window and step on the carpet, a series of pink and yellow roses come out of the ground, it is a magical world. There is music in the air. A flock of angels descends on you, and flies down to receive you. There is a divine ambience created by the holiness of the angels smiling at you"

"But where are you?" she opened her eyes and asked me.

"I am already there, walking behind you, holding you because you are the queen of that magical world. We are both dressed in white." I rested my hands on her waist.

"There is a magic wand in your hand. The wand can make your every wish come true. What will you wish for?" I asked her.

"I wish that you will stay with me and spend lots of time with me," she replied me.

"And?"

"I feel good."

"And?" I continued.

"And... I don't know. This is the only thing I can think of!"

"Can I hold you from behind?" I asked her.

"Yeah but please continue the story," she said. She loved being in the magical world of imagination.

"Those children are cherubs in the lap of angels. Angels are flying in the smoky clouds. Everything looks afloat in the silky white clouds including mountains, trees, flowers and vines wrapped around the golden rocks. Distant mountains look like the tip of an iceberg from which descends a milky waterfall which get lost in the aromatic smokes," and I slipped my hands around her waist and hugged her from behind.

"There is a big wooden house to your right with…" before I could continue further…

"Niam…!" she interrupted me.

"Yeah?" I replied.

"Are you afraid of spilling your heart out? I waited for you after that night camp every day but you were always shy and never spoke your heart out. Now, even when you talk, you would speak out your dream but through a story. You want to make me comfortable before you would hold me. I always said you don't need permission. Maybe, those words mean a lot, but I know that even when given total freedom, you would respect me. Don't be so afraid, everything is going to be awesome and as long as we are alive. There is always a possibility. Miracles do happen!" I held her tighter as she finished speaking.

"I don't know how this world works. I do not know how destiny affects life. But if you believe in the stars and those planetary configurations then, someday, sure your wish would be complete," I said.

"Come closer!" she said, and pressed herself close to me as though we were comparing heights.

I held her and she got onto my feet. We walked, foot-on-foot to the bed. She hugged me close and pressed her face to my chest. She had one hand around my neck and the other around my waist.

"I think I need some more wine," I said.

"Now? What? No more stories?" she looked little disappointed like a child who was not told the whole story on bed.

"Na, you were right. I wanted to express my dreams but you understood what I was saying. I don't know what to say now. One thing is sure. Destiny is not going to work for you unless you are not going to work towards your destiny!" I inched across the room to get myself some wine.

"You want some?"

"No," she said, clinging to me and her face buried in my chest. She had walked the distance to the wine, her feet still on mine.

"Okay. So are you going be this way all night?" I asked.

"Don't pretend as if you don't want me to be like this," she said.

"Then be there," I sipped my wine.

When I was done, I inched to the bed, she was still clinging to me. Candles had almost burnt down to their bottoms. Street lamps were also lost in the darkness of the raining night. The sound of the rain on the tin roof was loud. We were lost in the sea of loudness because there was nothing left for my eyes to perceive in the darkness thus, my body was heavily relying on my ears. The sound of the rain on the tin roof was loud. I ran my fingers over her cheeks. She looked at me and closed her eyes with pleasure. She acted in a delicate way like a touch-me-not plant. Our senses got synced into each other. My every touch was inducing a magic into her mind and over her body. I was pulling up the curtains of a stage set and she was rising up like the folded curtains to show more of what was on the other side of her.

Afloat were I and her, in the dark. A mystical mellifluous euphony was being played in the rhythm of the falling drops of rain. I lifted her face, and took a look at her speaking eyes. Her face shone little yellowish in the light coming through the window from the outside. She aligned her ears with my thumping heart.

My senses were losing control. Though I had an urge to kiss her but I felt myself like a happy child who was going to steal some chocolates but was still afraid of something even when there was no one at home. Her pull was a rub of a total sensation against my body. Her smell and her burning breaths over my neck, closer and deeper, were carrying me away. Short warm breaths, blood being pumped with large thumps, my heart was unable to contain blood. With the tightest ever hold, she was squeezed to me. Warmed with hug, the fire broke out of enamored ice and I held her lower lips in between my lips. Warm, soft, smooth to touch and I was imbibing the extracts of the sweetest fruit in the world.

"*Umm...mmm...mmm...mmm......mmm...mmm...*
...m....."

I pulled her up little more and I felt that the ribbon of her robe had fallen open suddenly but she did not care for that at all and neither she was in a mood to care for. Moments later, she was above me, knelt down over her elbows and knees, like a kid walking on four legs. I could feel the swipe of the helm of the robe on my legs as she knelt up. A waft of soft air wiped over my chest as she slowly came over me. The loose ribbon of the bathrobe was on the verge of losing its tie. As she leaned in, I could see the robe covering her back, from her neck to her hip. Though it was dark but still, it was easier for me to comprehend her curves and shape against little burning lights of Shimla in the background, being reflected on the glass window.

I moved my gaze along the distance from her neck to her hip. She was shaped like an inverted ceramic ewer with a rounded bottom and a V-shaped depression in the middle. She leaned in to kiss me. I felt the ribbon tickling my torso. It was so soothing that I wanted to close my eyes. I was trying hard to, but I could not close my eyes because she had just crept over me and I wanted to see her. For another moment, I again saw her curvy passage running along her back to her hip. As she leaned in more, I could see the wide openings of the robe converging together somewhere under her waist. Those two wide fronts were not loosely tied with the loose ribbon which was struggling hard to hold the two front openings together. If the ribbon had got released, more of her inner beauty could have got exposed. I saw her coming close to me. She looked into my eyes. I could not resist the temptation and closed my eyes, finally, in anticipation. At the very next moment, I felt a wet and soft feather swiped softly and slowly across my lips.

Before that soft feather could get away from my lips, I caught them in between my lips and a rave of saliva, tenderly glistened my lips. We were spilling our love out on each other. There was an infinite exchange of love. I would sometimes hold her lips in between my teeth softly and the way my teeth would glide over her lips when she would pull that away, would be shimmering to the smallest ripples in calm water.

The front plackets of that rob ran down her front like two hilly rivers. Her neck was like a vast plain curvature from where the rivers changed their courses. Both the rivers ran down her neck and mingled somewhere in the dark valley united by a single gorge. However, before mingling together the rivers passed through and ran along two beautiful hills. Those hills were like ripen mangoes in the hand of the creator. Between those hills, those two plackets met.

I opened my eyes and looked at her. Things were getting steamy. I held her in my arms. She pressed herself on me. I held her head and told her not move. Her lower lip was between my lips. That was the first time for me. I felt the energy that filled my body. With her lips now firmly pressed on mine, I closed my eyes. I tried to regain my senses. I closed her eyes with my palm and she laid over me silently. For a few moments, I felt like the center point of the whole of the energy of my body was wrapped at our lips. I moved the lump of the energy down my body in my mind. As she reached down to my chest, I felt the pulpiest sensation throughout my body.

I would rub her back and she would kiss me softly in return. She was enjoying my touch with her head resting immovable at my chest as if she wanted to rest there for her lifetime. She would get never hungry or thirsty when she was in the haven of my arms. Silence was still ruling the air and rain was still layering over our silence.

She was still lying over me. I was still moving my hand over her back.

"What happened?" I asked.

She moved her head a little and looked up at me. She had the same mystical look in her eyes – the one that I couldn't decipher. It was as though her eyes were telling me to find out the answers myself. I gazed into her eyes. She blinked once and buried her face in my chest.

"I do not want you to go away. I love you, Niam!" she said.

She looked into my eyes again, and I saw the clouds of sadness lingering about in her eyes. I was sure she had a lot on her mind that she wanted to tell me about – but couldn't say much for whatever reason. I couldn't hold back. Her single line revealed the most genuine truth of my existence.

"I love you very much, my girl from the woods!" I said, as I ran my hands along her arms.

That gave her a nudge and she would try to assimilate her existence into mine. Perhaps she was listening to my heart-beats; she was probing the flow of my blood to my heart. We didn't speak. Both of her hands were clangored around my chest as if she was not ready to let me go forever. I never felt her holding me so firm. If given a chance, she had even fought with the whole world for me; she had snatched me back even from death.

On one side of her was standing the potential determination while on another side was the reality. There was a fracas in her mind, a clash of reality and the potential future. Her innocent heart was unable to subsume the uncertainties and possible certainties at a single time. I could feel the strain and the same strain with which she was trying to be a part of me. The fray could be seen in her hold.

She was trying to hug me unbelievably firm. I could feel her clinch over my chest. It was so tight. The pressure built inside her had surmounted her mind.

"Are you ok?" the only thing I could say and it was like I let off the inundation out of her barrage.

Her fingers were dug deeply into my hair and she was kissing me so madly. I had never experienced that before. Her grip was so tight over my arms. I could see her eyes were wet. She lied over my face and kissed me but that time, she did not release me from her kiss.

"*Niam...!*" she took my name and did not move at all.

Tip! A drop of water had fallen over my cheek. Tip! There was another soaking up into the same drop. And, more drops followed the first two drops. They rolled down my cheek. I was confused if I was crying or she was crying. It was she. She was lying over me. I felt as if that trail of the tears had rolled out of my eyes and they slowly got lost somewhere in the darkness, never to return. Believe me, I felt them running down my cheek, I felt them getting lost in between our lips; you have to believe me that I felt the saline taste when the tears touched her lips too.

I felt like I had seen the divine face of love. I was flying, I was not aware if this was a dream or if it was all really happening. The last thing I remembered was that she was lying beside me, holding me. I rubbed her back. I don't remember when we fell asleep.

Next day, when I opened my eyes, the sun was already shining on my face through the window. I could not open my eyes and look out of the window because of the glare. The curtains were drawn back since the last night. I turned around lazily in bed, looking for her. I couldn't see her anywhere.

"*Siya!* Are you around?" There was no reply.

I opened the window to look out. The Gypsy was still in its place and the dog sitting beside it. I suddenly grew wide awake and rushed down to ask the guard if he had seen her. He told me that he had gotten up late that day because of the party. He had not seen her going by. I was surprised. I decided to go to the market to see if she was there – I did just that, driving in the Gypsy in my night suit. I didn't find her there, and so drove straight to the town, to her hut. It was empty. There was no sign that someone lived there just a day ago. I went back to collect my things and then went to the Hotel. I asked about Siya and her mother, but no one had any clue. I went to some of the shops we visited together. I asked the porters and the store owners. Some confirmed that they did see them, but a few days ago. I searched every nook and cranny in the hope of finding her.

By the time it was evening, I realized I did not have much time to spare. I had to leave for Kalka. I returned to the cottage, where Raam Singh was already eagerly waiting for me. I asked him to look out for them and return to me within an hour. I packed my luggage. Raam Singh returned with no news. We left the cottage, to depart for Kalka in the Gypsy. While crossing Shimla, I looked out of the window, searching every place with my eyes to find her, but in vain. Sometimes, our hopes cling onto things that seem familiar, but are not what we are looking for. When we left Shimla behind, I lost all hopes.

After crossing the border, Raam Singh said, "Sir, it is strange that you couldn't find her."

"Yeah," I said.

"She must have gone to some relatives' place. But no one carries all their things with them for that. There were no plans of them moving away to a different place, either. It's really strange," Raam Singh

"Yeah," I said.

"I don't know... She could have at least let you know. It was very abrupt!"

"Yeah," I replied.

"Sir, I suppose it is their decision. We are not to decide for them." I nodded to this part of his conversation.

We reached Kalka.

"Sirji, keep coming. Remember me! I will come for you. All the taxi guys know me here and will leave you at Shimla any day, at any time! " he said, and drove off.

Old Lady in the Train

Kalka was not worse than Shimla. The sun was brighter and the winds were warmer, too. Sitting on a wooden bench in the sun, I thought about her. Behind me, the toy train stood on the platform. I looked at the happy faces of the tourists who were excited to leave for Shimla. I felt as though I shared some connection with the train. They were the same trains I crossed while driving around Shimla. I wanted to be one of those tourists. In front of me was standing a broad-gauge train. There was a huge difference across the thirty feet of the platform. While the small gauge left for only Shimla, the broad gauge connected Kalka to all of the India. One carried the tourists and other carried the memories.

I entered the train. It was another world altogether. The iron bars on the windows, the heat, the conversation that people had, the crowd - and all of it made me feel like this was a whole different world. I got onto the train and kept my luggage under the seat. I looked at the Kalka-Shimla toy train standing across us, on the tracks. I was caged inside my train and across the platform was freedom in the form of the train to happiness.

Later, an old couple got into the same compartment. Nothing seemed interesting to me and so, I decided to sit by the window and look outside. Slowly the train rolled on the rails and Kalka station was drifting away slowly in the opposite direction. The empty wooden seats on the platforms, the hills far away, the happy faces moving away: all signified that the show was over.

"*Welcome to the world of reality again*," I said to myself. I wondered where she was. I couldn't forget our last night together – I couldn't forget her at all. Everything I looked at now reminded me of her. I did not expect her to appear in front of me out of thin air. She was now a memory. I had to be tough and let her go.

I bought some magazines and tried to focus on them. Sometimes, I got down when the train stopped for the pass, for another train and smoke or take some pictures.

The lady sitting opposite me seemed interested in me. We began to chat. I told her about my work. She and her husband loved travelling and were returning after a month-long journey that took them to the Himachal. I began sharing my photographs. She became more curious. She was impressed by the kind of work I was into. She was not the first one to be impressed, though. Somehow, she was also able to read into the agony that rested in my mind. She was experienced and must have sensed my dilemma while I explained the pictures and told her about the places where I went with her. I was relieved, but it was still not over. The old lady smiled. She bought me a cup of tea and offered me some snacks from the Shimla Bakery.

"Son, are you missing someone in particular?" she asked me. I decided I wouldn't lie.

"Yeah! I met a girl and I lost her before leaving Shimla," I said.

"Were you in love with each other?" she asked. Her question was straightforward and intriguing all the same. I couldn't help but admire her for her candor.

"Yeah, I liked her lot but, we did not express our love to each other," I said.

She went silent for some time. We heard the sounds of the train as it snaked through the tracks.

I continued after a while. "Maybe we did have many chances to share – but the fact is that I was not going to stay permanently and had to return from Shimla anyway. I was in a dilemma," I confessed, evidently in need of someone to spill my heart out. I was still not able to express it aloud because the journey was never complete.

"You know what, son!" she began.

"One's eyes never lie. See those eyes," she said as she pointed to her husband.

"They never lie. We are still in love. I see the same love in his eyes years after our marriage and the same love in your eyes too." I smiled at her.

We were going to the same city, and spent the rest of the journey talking to each other. She had almost convinced me that I was in love. I had no counter-argument. After sharing my story with the old lady, I thought I would feel better, but she had complicated the situation further I could see evidently that I was in love, and so was the girl, with me. It had an abrupt ending. I could do nothing about it. I wished I could go back in time. I had started to miss her even more. But there was no hope left, now that I was occupied with work and such else. I felt like I was sitting in a dark corner under the dark night. I wanted to hide somewhere though there was no one around to see me. I was counting on to the hopes left. I began believing in miracles. I was counting on possibilities and it all seemed workable. I had a plan in mind. After a week of work, I would ask for a vacation and come back here to search for her. Where would I begin the search, though? Whom would I ask? Seeing me in distress with my thoughts, the old lady tried to distract me.

Soon, the journey came to an end. The train entered the city. This was where I worked. There were big houses, tall buildings and people running about in a hurry. The sight of big glasshouses, local trains filled with thousands of people, huts lining the sides of railway tracks – it all scared me. Humanity had left us a long time ago, and was watching us from a distance. I was back at the place that earned me my bread and butter. The train came to a halt. I helped the old lady and her husband out onto the platform. Their son and his wife were waiting for them at the station. I accompanied them to their son's car. Just as the old lady sat inside, she called me closer and whispered into my ears,

"Son! If your love was true, she will return to you in any form. She must be feeling the same as you are feeling now. The world will exert any amount of pressure to see the two true lovers together. Believe me!" She kissed me on my right cheek.

Their car sped off into the distance. I stood rooted to the spot. People crossed and passed me by the dozen, uncaring about my presence.

"Don't let your hopes die. The whole world runs on hope!" I remembered her words as she smiled and waved her through the window.

Solitude and Me

I returned to the office the next morning. I decided not to meet too many people except for a few of my close friends. I was on leave until the coming Friday. Fridays has always been an important day of my life. It would be the day when I would present my work after returning from shoot-trips. I met my friends on the corner of a street over *chai-sutta* (tea and a smoke). I was very grateful for the great set of friends I had. They were my source of motivation and stood by me in lean times.

"*Saale, mara hua kyun lag raha hai?*" one of them asked me, translating to mean why I looked like I was dead. Another passed a lighter to me. I lit my cigarette and drew a deep puff. I looked at all of them in turn and exhaled the smoke.

"I am tired," I said, not wanting to prolong the topic. My friends decided that we would sit together for drinks later that evening – but the idea of drinking did not excite me.

"I am leaving on a vacation this evening with my family. I just came here to tell you guys this," I lied through my teeth.

We had agreed to meet on Friday and have fun, they were okay with what I said and didn't ask me anything. I tended to live a life of solitary confinement in my apartment. Sometimes, I would drive to a church nearby to sit alone there. No one cared to come there on weekdays. I knew I was killing myself inside with this imposition of solitude.

At my apartment, my bedroom window opened to a vast lake and woods. I would draw back the curtains and put on some soft music and spend my time staring up at the ceiling. In the evenings, I would look at the setting sun against the lake and the birds flying by. I had purposely settled for that apartment only for the view, but I did not find it attractive at all. I needed someone to talk to, and I had lost the courage to share things with others.

While driving to the church, I would decide to confess everything to the priest there, but I would gradually lose my courage on the way. In the night, I would turn on the small blue light bulb just to fill my room with light. The curtains would remain in place. The pillow wouldn't move an inch and I would only step out of the building for a pack of smokes or some eatables. I enjoyed my solitude and the lone company of my pain.

Sometimes, I gathered enough courage to ask the priest if I could make a confession, but I never confessed anything. He understood my dilemma. He was a seasoned person at his profession and had seen hundreds like me each week. I would wind up sitting on the front bench, seeking peace in seeing the Lord for a long time. I loved the peace and the silence there. The bell would chime every hour.

The priest was mostly busy reading a book or writing something in his log. When I sat longer, sometimes, he would join me. We would sit together in silence. I had no courage to look into the eyes of a holy man. But when he was around me, I found a solace descending on me. His spirituality was soothing and comforting. He neither forced me to confess and nor was I interested in letting him know my past. But I loved having him around me. Though I could not talk, I felt his presence and it felt like peace around me.

Gradually, the days passed and it was Friday. I had to share my experience with the staffs at office. Friday would mostly be a party day and people were invariably free, which went well with their curiosity since they were eager to know about the story behind all my photographs. People were always interested in stories. At my workplace, I had a few admirers too. I had already sent a lot of photographs by post to the office while still in Shimla. The photos had already inspired discussions among a few. I enjoyed their expressions. The girls were amazed at the colors and the natural beauty. I confess they were lesser interested in abstracts and the emotions. People had their own choices. Around lunchtime on the days I returned, I would be congratulated and asked to share my stories. I enjoyed having people sit around my table and listen to me like children listening to a story. The Fridays on which I returned was dedicated to me and my presence in office, until I left to party with my friends. But that Friday, I was not confident. Earlier, I used to feel elated before I went on the stage to make presentations of my photography. I would spend all night picking out the best shots. But I dreaded that Friday. I did not feel like working. I was not afraid of presenting my work, it was just that my mind was full of other things. I decided to approach it with a blank mind and wing it at the venue. But, nothing happens the way you plan it, for destiny has its own plans.

The Girl From the Woods

Friday arrived. I showered in warm water, dressed in my suit and polished my shoes and left to office. The party began after lunch. After eating and another round of *chai-sutta*, I sneaked out of the group of friends that had gathered to chat, and entered the presentation hall from the back door. I took a look at the empty chairs. It was scary. I disliked crowds. I imagined what the hall would be like when it was filled up. But I had seen such crowds in the past and I consoled myself that I could do it. It was just a matter of an hour or two.

Slowly, people started walking in. I went backstage, where I was supposed to enter from. I heard the murmur of people talking as they walked in and sat down in some of the empty seats. There were crunching sounds of the seats and shoes shuffling. The microphones were being checked and projectors were being tested. There were a few workers backstage trying to fit things into their proper places. Some smiled, some shook hands, some took their hands out but were too shy to shake mine, and some would look at me and go back to their work. I felt like I was on display, kept hidden before the grand unveiling.

Before the program began, I met a young man. He told that he was the new office-boy who handled administration. The murmur in the hall had slackened down. It appeared that the Masters of Ceremonies had arrived on stage. There was a hush. I heard footsteps. With each step, my heart beat faster. I was trying to calm myself.

The program began. People came on stage. Applause echoed across the hall. The introduction was over. A few more guests entered. I was more or less focused on nothing, until they announced my name. I did not have the courage to face so many people at one go. I froze for an instant. I felt cold, but I had to move. I got a glimpse of the hall from the corner of the stage as I entered. The once empty hall now felt warmer. People were smiling at me from the front. Whistles where blown and applause sounded out. I felt a surge of energy. I was smiling but I had no idea where I was or what I was going to do. I started arranging the slides at the projector. There was complete silence. Tons of lights focused on me while the rest of the hall was dark. I did not want to be the center of attraction but I was. The slider clicked. There was a black and white picture of a young girl in the woods.

"Any guesses folks?" I asked, as I turned around.

"The background looks like it is from the Second World War and the lady is Polish or Jewish," said an old man from the second row. There was a suppressed round of laughter. I smiled at his response.

"Any more guesses?" I asked again, my voice echoed in the hall.

There were thousands of thoughts in people's minds. Some compared the background of the photograph with the Second World War due to the woods and the lone lady in a long black overcoat. Some said it related to poverty. Some found the woods very lonely but no one could find the love in black and white world.

"Okay. I will tell you about this photograph in the end," I said, and clicked the slider on to the second picture.

The second picture floated across the screen. It was from the set on celestial photography. I kept the camera rolling. There were all kinds of pictures. The audience chimed in with applause, gasps of astonishment and appreciation. They loved it, especially the lower Bazaar, the rising sun, the snow fields and the camp night celestial display. There were two dozen photographs, and I lingered on some of them – the ones that reminded me of her. The emotions and the memories that fuelled the stories I told about her left people spellbound. Each photograph had me grow emotional. It was slowly growing harder and harder for me to remain in the present. My memories were pulling me into the past constantly. There was a war inside my mind. I was not able to resist myself when the memories revisited me after every photograph. I did not know how I looked to the audience – but I did realize that the emotions that the photographs portrayed, moved everyone. I managed to finish my speech. My eyes stared into the darkness beyond the stage, and then I turned to the screen. I managed to sound happy when I finished the presentation. It was customary to reveal the theme of the photography at the end of the function. I had to stand in the spotlight and do just that. But before that I had to wait for the function to come to an end. I stood behind the curtain – it was dimply lit. The world forgets the photographers soon, but the photographs remain leaving a bigger footprint on their minds. After I spoke, there were a few rounds of speeches from guests at the event. I left the stage and stood behind it, I saw the young lad approach me again – he had some envelopes in his hand.

"Sir, these are all the mails you received for the past month," he handed me a bunch of letters.

I heard the audience applauding. It didn't frighten me anymore. I looked through the envelopes. Most had shiny envelopes in random colors – I just skimmed past them. I stopped at one: a plain, blue colored envelope. It didn't have a sender's name and address.

Suddenly, hope took over my heart – I wished it was her. The next moment, the thought of the old lady on the train lingered on my mind. I hastily opened the letter. I glanced through it from top to bottom. My name was announced on stage, it had come to the last part of the presentation. I approached the stage, still holding the letter in my left hand. I heard the silence in the hall. The black-and-white picture was shown on the screen. Everyone was waiting for me to reveal the theme of the photography and the story behind the photograph. I walked over to the mike. I felt everyone's eyes on me. I heard my feet thudding on the stage. I heard the letter swish as it touched my shirt while I walked. I reached the mike.

"This time, I am not going to name the theme. Some themes are too complex to be named. Nonetheless, I would like to read something to you all. It is a little longer than I intended, but I hope you will enjoy it as much as I will - because we are both unaware of what has been written on this paper," I raised the letter in the air.

"I know that it's the party that remains on people's minds. Some of our friends are even getting late." I said, and there was laughter in the hall.

"Yeah, the party is on everyone's mind, but, if you just promise me five minutes of your time, I promise you a month of my interesting stay in the woods, from a stranger," I put the letter under the reading light. It rustled in front of the mike and the rustle echoed across the hall. There was complete silence and I began reading:

"*Dear Niam,*

It's me. I wonder how and from where I should start. You entered my life out of nowhere and suddenly my life had turned so beautiful. For a moment, I thought my life had changed and I had met a part of myself that was unknown to me. Not only had I found a lost part of me, but I also found my lost world and my father in you. Your presence always reminded me of him. In your care and protection, I found the affection of my father. Walking, holding your finger, almost made me believe that God had given my father back to me through you. I was fortunate enough to know you, to be with you, to experience such beautiful moments with you. I never knew that the same mountains, valley, and the flowing stream could be more beautiful and divine. But it was, when you were there with me. Drinking hot tea, standing in the hut and watching the cold winter rain falling from the gloomy skies above - had all paused the time for me. I was so lost with you, that I sipped the hot tea within moments and never realized that I could do that. You never spoke much, but your eyes did the talking. I never knew that so much could be shared just, by not even uttering a single word, when you have someone who captures your feelings even in silence, through a pair of silent eyes."

The words echoed. I wondered if she was standing and looking at me as I read this out. Everything just flashed before my eyes as if the words were being framed into the pictures while I was speaking and my past was happily smiling at me. The hall was still dark. It was just me in the past with her.

"I never knew that a hug and a kiss from someone who was unknown to you until yesterday could make me so happy. I never knew that resting on a shoulder could bring me the love and affection that a mother's lap alone can give. I had no idea that speaking to someone heretofore a stranger, would make me feel like I had found my soul's lost half. Looking at you was like looking at me. I wanted to feel how I looked in your eyes. Self-obsession and craziness, right? But I saw your eyes in my eyes. I felt more beautiful than ever, it was as if I had been born again. I felt I was a part of all your emotions. I had read about it in books, but I had never realized that someone can become such a great part of another's existence until I met you in person. I never realized that the dreams that I had dreamt of, could turn into reality until you came by. It's every girl's dream that she is cherished by her man. I was so blessed to have you by my side. But all that – all of that, was just so we would part one day! Why is life so unfair? Why does one have to be snatched away just when their dreams seem to be turning into reality? The beautiful world soon becomes a complex reality and it is impossible to face so many hurdles"

I could feel that the same enigma had perturbed the whole crowd. I could see at the faces; in the long run, we all were riding the same boat of life

"It is very true that love may happen at the first sight, and even in a second. But letting that go takes a lifetime. At times, even one life is not enough and you don't mind taking infinite number of births in this mundane world when it comes to being with the one who completes you in every possible ways.

The last few days prior to your departure were very difficult for me. I was always fighting my emotions and thoughts. I wondered how I would face you, how I would stay without you. I wondered how and when the same rain would become special to me again. I had rediscovered myself in you. I felt the protection that a child finds in his mother's womb and in a father's arms. How will it be when you won't be by my side? All the moments spent with you always led me to our imaginary paradise. I never felt so much connected to your soul before your every touch, touched and absorbed my soul. I felt like my soul and body belonged to you. I wanted to surrender myself to you. You were always careful about me; you tried not to disclose your feelings. But your eyes never lied. Whatever we had seen in each other's eyes revealed what we each were aware of. I was always scared of losing you, and I know you were scared of losing me, too, because we know that some people are too precious, and they are meant to be with you only for a short time. I guess it's true that some people create the most beautiful memories in life together, but are not meant to be together forever because forever is too long to sustain. Some people come into your life, give meaning to your existence and let you meet a hidden part of yourself. But they have to part ways with you just like the sky and the sea look beautiful together yet they are never meant for each other."

It was getting harder for me to continue. It felt like I was bipolar or something – one part of me had travelled into the past and another part was left in the present. The big hall, the large crowd, the deep silence and the illuminated stage all felt insignificant for me. I felt like my identity was challenged. I felt like I was still a part of the crowd, but standing at a distance and not standing where I was. My endeavor to rise above society was meaningless if I was returning to the same society again and again. I wondered why I was standing there. What was I doing? But, I managed to continue-

"*That rainy night, the cottage and its French windows looked like something out of the world. Had I known that something could have existed, I would have prayed to have paused all those priceless moments forever so we could remain locked in them forever. Your charming smile and the way you looked at me meant everything to me. A girl finds her world concealed in the eyes of her man and those eyes never lie. Your eyes took me to a different world; a world which is was so true, pure and divine, like your heart and it can never be wrong. It is true that some people touch the heart, and still others, touch our souls: just like you did.*

Oh, Niam! The last two months were like a dream. When dreams come true, we get carried away and don't realize that our life has changed so much. At the same time, when you see the same dream drifting away, you feel so helpless and miserable. You don't have the courage to just let it go because there is so much in it to let go off.

You know how hard it is to wear a genuine smile when there is a deep surge of sorrow hidden inside the heart. Letting go was never easy for me because I never believed in separation. Loved ones always stay in our hearts forever even in their absence. I learned this, and have felt this over the years especially after my father left us. Yet, some people are meant to meet, create great memories and then part ways. I have never understood it, and I still don't understand it. What I know is that I want you to be happy always and be the same person like you are now. You deserve much more than happiness. You are a priceless gem. You brought happiness and joy to my barren soul and made me feel so special. In the course of this, I did not realize it, or maybe, I did not want to realize it, either.

Everything in Shimla will remind me of you. I believe in miracles and will never lose faith in them.

I didn't have the courage to stay there any longer. I left without notifying you. I did not have the courage to put up a smile when I was dying inside with the thought of separating from you. It's none of our faults, though.

One moment is enough to fall in love, but it takes years to picture a life in love. Do not feel too bad about it, please. Our story was a part of destiny and you were the perfect example of a wonderful strange traveler. You will be a great husband one day and you wife will be lucky. I have moved to a new place where I have a new job as a teacher.

If a traveller is meant to cross the same road again, I will wait for the horseman every sunset on the dusty trails of these hills.

Niam! You are the best man I have come across since my father. I wish you all the happiness in your life, because seeing you happy again will give me happiness."

I love you Niam!

I will always love you.

Yours',

The Girl from the Woods, Sanawar.

A Note on the Author

Amar Shekhar is cofounder of an adventure-based company, Hardyhawks adventures. He writes his adventure experiences over his blog trekkerpedia.com. This book is inspired from real-life incidents as an adventurer and a trek organizer.

He has a master's degree in Information Technology from IIIT-Bangalore. When not found writing, he is busy shooting the nature.

To get in touch with Amar via:

Facebook: https://www.facebook.com/amar.shekhar

Twitter Handle: AmarShekhar26

Blog: http://trekkerpedia.com

Email: amar.shekhar2005@gmail.com

"We are so different yet we are so similar"

That's what they say to each other when an **adventurer** meets a girl living aloof from society.

A lot of fireworks happen when two different worlds, Niam, a passionate photographer and a girl, firm believer in **"real love"**, meet accidently in Shimla and fall in love. Two lonely souls envelop each other like there is no end to the **journey** of their lives. Time starts shaping up the congruency of their spirits. Love and passion get in ethereal sync like they were meant to complete each other.

"What are you going to do after you leave from here?"

To which Niam has no answers when asked by the girl. His passion, her love, **spirituality**, their reputations, everything becomes so entangled that Niam needs to decide his fate between **passion** and love, or both.

So, does a soul seeking spiritual solace, finally decide to embrace what's called a **"relationship"** of this mundane world? Does the real love of the **girl** manage to thrive together with free flying soul? Or, they just wither away altogether?